What Good Girls Do

Jonathan Butcher

Also by Jonathan Butcher:

THE CHOCOLATEMAN

Further reading by the Sinister Horror Company:

THE BAD GAME – Adam Millard

BURNING HOUSE – Daniel Marc Chant
MALDICION – Daniel Marc Chant
MR. ROBESPIERRE – Daniel Marc Chant
AIMEE BANCROFT AND THE SINGULARITY STORM –
Daniel Marc Chant
INTO FEAR - Daniel Marc Chant

BITEY BACHMAN – Kayleigh Marie Edwards

TERROR BYTE – J. R. Park
PUNCH – J. R. Park
UPON WAKING – J. R. Park
THE EXCHANGE – J. R. Park

POSTAL – J. R. Park & Matt Shaw

GODBOMB! – Kit Power
BREAKING POINT – Kit Power

KING CARRION – Rich Hawkins

MARKED – Stuart Park

THE BLACK ROOM MANUSCRIPTS VOL 1 – Various
THE BLACK ROOM MANUSCRIPTS VOL 2 – Various

*Visit SinisterHorrorCompany.com for further information on these and
other titles.*

SINISTER
HORROR
COMPANY

PRESENTS

WHAT
GOOD
GIRLS
DO

JONATHAN
BUTCHER

WHAT GOOD GIRLS DO

First Published in 2017

Copyright © Jonathan Butcher 2017

Published by The Sinister Horror Company

Photography by Sian Jansen-Bowen

Additional cover design by Vincent Hunt
www.jesterdiablo.blogsport.co.uk
Twitter: @jesterdiablo

ISBN: 978-0-9935926-2-1

ACKNOWLEDGEMENTS

First thanks goes to my parents for their constant support – even though I hope they never read this filth.

To my fellow horror scribes (Justin Park, Daniel Marc Chant, Matty-Bob Cash, Duncan Ralston, Theresa Derwin, Jim McLeod, Duncan Bradshaw…) who have offered me opportunities, advice, and even friendship.

To Sian, for helping with the presentation of *What Good Girls Do*, to Kyna, for answering unpleasant medical questions and additional help, to Emily, for kindly modelling for the book, and to everyone who gave me feedback in the story's early stages.

To teachers and friends who have recognised and encouraged my passion for writing over the years, helping me become the depraved storyteller I am today.

And finally, to anyone who reads (and hopefully reviews!) *What Good Girls Do*: whether you like it or loathe it, *thank you*.

This story is dedicated to abusers and coercers everywhere.
I dream of merciless, agonizing karma for each of you.

"To live is to suffer, to survive is to find some meaning in the suffering."

Friedrich Nietzche

"You can do anything. Grab them by the pussy."

Donald Trump, President of the United States

1. Girl

The Daddy on the screen says: "Yeah, that's it. I wanna see you puke."

And My Daddy says to me: "That's what Good Girls do, isn't it?"

And I say: "Yes, Daddy."

I've seen it all before. I'm always watching the Girls cocksuck the Daddies, and when My Daddy tells me that I should do it too, I get down on my knees like a Good Girl should.

The Daddy on the screen makes the Girl on the screen puke with his big cock. It is bigger than My Daddy's, but My Daddy manages to make me puke, too, all over my tits.

When I'm done, I cough and wipe my mouth, and look up at My Daddy with his big face and fluffy grey hair.

My Daddy says: "It's a special day, Girl. You've gotta be extra sweet, coz I'm gonna let you meet some of your other Daddies again. You like that, don't you? Yes."

He goes to the big door in My Room and puts the key into it. It goes CLA-CLUNK.

My Daddy says, "You're such a Good Girl, sweetie," and leaves again.

When it's just me alone in My Room, I go to the bathroom and drink some water to make the dirty taste go away and then I sit on my bed. I decide to scratch the Bad away for a while until my arms are all red, and then I do some exercise. When I'm all warm and sweaty and better, I lie on my bed and look over at Daddy's Eye.

Daddy's Eye is on the wall above the door to My Room. It is square and about the same size as my foot, and it has a red dot that blinks on-and-off, on-and-off, and a little round screen.

My Daddy says, "I'm always looking out for you, even when you can't see me." He says, "Sometimes, *all the Daddies* are looking out for you."

I look up at the ceiling pipes and the light bulb. I shiver. I wish I had clothes like My Daddy because it gets cold down here, but My Daddy says, "Good Girls don't wear clothes."

Sometimes, when it's just me, I look at the books that Daddy gives me. They have words that Daddy showed me how to read, but I don't know what some of them mean, like "airplane" and "office" and "sky". Mostly, though, they're about fucking. I'm writing my own book, too.

Sometimes, I watch the films that Daddy gives me. They show Daddies doing all the things to their Girls that My Daddy does to me. They teach me how to be a Good Girl.

If I ever ask My Daddy where all the other Girls are, like the ones in the films, My Daddy just tells me, "Don't be silly."

"Don't be silly," he says. "Don't be silly."

Sometimes, I think that there used to be another Girl here too, a bigger Girl. I think that she used to hug me and keep me warm, but I don't think she wanted to fuck me. I once told Daddy about this, but he got shaky and left My Room without even saying "Don't be silly." He kept my light on for ages so I couldn't sleep, and he stopped giving me food. He didn't come back until I banged and banged and banged on the door.

When he came back, I was really tired and really hungry. I said, "Please please please, don't do that again." My Daddy cried and said that he wouldn't do it again, and then he put his cock inside me and said, "You like that don't you," and I said, "Yes, Daddy."

Today, while I'm looking at Daddy's Eye, I start to feel shaky and different again, so I get up and sit on the floor and watch one of the films.

"Show me that tight asshole," the Daddy on the screen says. "Good girl."

There's another Daddy with him. They stand at different ends of the Girl and fuck her tight asshole and her nice smooth cunt and her mouth. They choke her and laugh and spit on her, and then they cum on her and then the screen goes black. Then two other Daddies appear with another Girl, and it all starts over again.

Lately, I haven't been reading or watching much, because I've started to feel shaky and different. It started when I watched the Other Film.

The Other Film's box looks just like the others: it shows a Girl with no clothes on. But when I watched it when My Daddy wasn't here, instead of seeing Daddies fucking and hurting their Girls like the normal films, I saw a Girl speaking with another Girl.

They talked about Daddies. They called them "men". They said that Daddies were Bad, and that when they put their big cocks into the Girls' nice smooth cunts, sometimes the Girls don't like it. They said that Daddies shouldn't fuck Girls like they do, and that if a Girl says "No," it means that the Daddy should stop. Then the Girls kissed and it made me feel funny.

In the Other Film, when the Girls left their room, there were big things and small things and a little furry thing with four legs called a dog and lots and lots of cars, which I've read about in some of my books. When the Girls found some other Daddies, the Girls were Bad. They made red stuff come out of the Daddies, and that made them fall asleep.

I don't think that My Daddy knows about the Other Film. I don't think he would like it.

But I can't stop thinking about it.

2. Serenity

I watch through our kitchen's delivery hatch as my little survivor Phillip tussles with his toddling twin sister Lilith on the living room floor. Phillip weeps half-heartedly as Lilith looms above him, giggling and pushing his shoulders into the carpet with her pudgy hands.

My husband Stuart, showered but still in his blue pyjamas, stands at the window on the far side, surveying the neighbourhood. On Saturdays, like today, our street takes longer to wake up than during the week, when it is a constant tide of cars and people coming and going.

Stuart's stocky frame is a silhouette before the morning sun that burns behind the glass. "Stop crying, Phillip," he mutters. "Are you *really* going to let my princess get the better of you?"

The twins roll sideways, reversing their positions.

Phillip starts to chuckle and Lilith's laughter crumbles into frustrated tears. They'll probably need their nappies changing after their scrap, and then our older son Declan will bathe them before we head out to the theme park.

While Declan supervises them bathing, I'm hoping that Stuart and I can have some fun of our own.

Phillip clambers between his sister's legs, cackling as he pins her. He breaks wind with a gentle squeak. Their eyes lock in identical sibling surprise and they chuckle in unison; too young for a conversation, but old enough to see the hilarity of a good fart.

The oven's digital clock tells me it's just a few minutes until 10am, when my firstborn has agreed to be woken and dragged from his blankety crypt.

I head through to the lounge, where my husband Stuart is still standing at the window. I'm happy to see that my little survivor Phillip remains on top of his sister Lilith, squeezed between her thighs.

At Stuart's side, I ask, "Did you print off the Castle Land vouchers? We need to make sure that…"

Without even turning, Stuart grabs a handful of hair from the back of my scalp. I gasp, closing my eyes and letting my head fall back. "Stuart, not in front of the…"

"Ssshhhh…they're playing."

I hear one giggle and one sob from the twins behind me, and then submit to a helpless warm rush. I lose myself to the darkness of my own eyelids, and when I open my eyes Stuart has turned towards me. A smile plays across his lips and his teeth glow against the beige of his freshly-shaven cheeks. "Honey. You have nothing to worry about."

My legs shudder, threatening to give way.

"Relax," he soothes, pulling my hair harder.

Out of view from the children, his other hand climbs the soft mound of my belly and cups my right breast. I want to remind him that we're standing at the window and that anyone might see, but when he squeezes my nipple to a halfway a point between pleasure and sharp pain I merely bite my lip. His hand glides over to my left breast and gives its tip a similarly harsh pinch.

"Go and wake Declan," Stuart says.

"Yes sir," I breathe, warming to the familiar role.

This is going to be a *fine* morning.

Jonathan Butcher

3. Girl

I don't want to be a Bad Girl, but while I'm watching the film today I get shaky and different. I want the Daddies in the film to stop doing what Daddies do.

I once said to My Daddy, "I don't feel Good today. I feel different."

When I said that, My Daddy told me, "It's okay, sweetie. *Things* can be Bad, but *feelings* can't. That means that Good Girls can feel Good, but they can't feel Bad – they can only feel different. So there's nothing to worry about, is there?"

And I said, "No, Daddy."

That's why I sometimes have to scratch my arms until I don't feel so different anymore, because I've scratched the Bad away.

When the Daddies in today's film start biting the new Girl's tits, I pull the disc out of the machine. I take it to the toilet and shut the door and drop the disc in the water and flush.

I have a film where a Daddy puts a Girl's head into the toilet and flushes it while he fucks her nice smooth cunt. The Daddy says, "Stay still, whore," and he pulls her hair and spanks her and fucks her tight ass.

My Daddy always says, "That's what Good Girls and Daddies do," but when I think about it today it makes me feel really, really different.

Even though it makes me feel like a Bad Girl, I get the Other Film from under my bed and put it into the machine.

I skip to the bit where the Girls are talking together, when they kiss and they say that Daddies shouldn't fuck Girls like they do. They say that Girls should only like other Girls, and then they kiss again. Then there's the bit when they find the first Daddy, and tell him that they want to fuck him. When the Daddy gets out his big hard cock, one of the Girls bites it until red stuff comes out. The Daddy screams, but the other Girl hits his head with a TV. There is loads and loads more red stuff and then the Daddy goes to sleep.

Something in My Room goes CLA-CLUNK.

I turn.

My Daddy opens the door. When he sees me, he looks shaky and really, REALLY different. His face looks like it does when he cums, and he says: "WHAT ARE YOU DOING?"

I tell him, "I'm sorry I'm sorry I'm sorry," even though I don't feel sorry.

When My Daddy comes over, he looks like he is going to break me, but he doesn't.

The Daddy on the TV is lying down, covered in red

stuff.

My Daddy bends over and switches the TV off, but because I feel even shakier and even more different, I jump up and push his face into the screen, really, really hard.

The screen breaks with a CRUK and My Daddy says: "Ah!"

When My Daddy stands up, a bit of the screen is stuck in his head and his face is all red and drippy. He tries to spank my face because I've been a Bad Girl, but I step away. He can't see me because of the red stuff in his eyes.

He has left the door to My Room open and I think about running through it and outside for the first time ever. My Daddy grabs my hair, though, like he sometimes does when he fucks me. He pulls me around to face him and screams, "WHAT DID YOU DO, GIRL?"

I've never felt this shaky and different before.

My Daddy rips my hair upwards, really hard, so I throw my hand out and hit the bit of broken screen that's stuck in his head. Even though it hurts me, I think it hurts My Daddy more.

Daddy lets go of my hair. He wobbles and looks like he is going to fall down. He reaches up and touches the bit of screen in his head. As he does, I bend over like a Good Girl getting her tight ass fucked, but instead of getting fucked I pick up the TV with both hands. It doesn't feel at all heavy when I lift it above me.

My Daddy makes his cum-face again. I drop my arms. The TV hits his head, really, really hard. It goes KSSSHHHH.

My Daddy shouts, and then he stops shouting, and then he falls down with the TV still on his head. He stops

11

moving. There is broken screen and red stuff all around him. It makes me think about the Daddy in the Other Film, the first one who falls asleep and doesn't wake up.

I suddenly feel different again.

REALLY different.

My arms are shaking, just like one of Daddy's buzzing toys that he sometimes fucks me with. I feel like I'm going to puke again. I think about scratching the Bad away, or having a shower, or going to sleep, but I just stand there, looking down at My Daddy. He isn't moving, not even a bit.

If he doesn't wake up, where will I get my food? And who will fuck my mouth and my nice smooth cunt and my tight asshole? Daddy always says, "That's what Good Girls do," and even though I don't like it, I still do it because I want to be a Good Girl.

I squeeze and pinch Daddy's legs. He doesn't move. I rub his cock but it doesn't get hard.

I say: "Wake up, Daddy, wake up."

I push the TV off his head. It goes KUNCH.

I want to slap My Daddy to wake him up, but there's more bits of screen sticking out of his face now, and there's so much red stuff over him that I can hardly see his skin. It makes me think of the film where the ten Daddies spit on and cum on a Girl's head, and the Girl ends up covered in white stuff. The stuff that's all over My Daddy is red, though, and it isn't thick or bubbly.

I decide to copy what the Girl does in the Other Film. Maybe that will wake him.

I unzip My Daddy's trousers and pull his cock out, and then bite it. I chew and I chew until his cock tastes different and it's all red and a different shape.

Still nothing.

When I am finished, I spit a few times and drink some water in the bathroom. Then, because I don't know what to do, but My Daddy isn't here to stop me, I pick up a green crayon and a red crayon from my desk and I scribble all over the walls, circling My Room until I get to the door that leads outside. It is still open, and when I drop the crayons and look at it I feel like I'm going to fall over again.

I wonder, where are all the other Girls and the other Daddies?

"Don't be silly," My Daddy always says, if I ever ask him. "Don't be silly."

But My Daddy's sleeping now, so he can't tell me not to be silly.

I ignore how shaky I am and go to the door.

Jonathan Butcher

4. Serenity

"Declan!" I call, for what feels like the trillionth time. "Will you *please* get up and help the twins with their bath? We're going to be late!"

Despite this morning's aggravation, Declan is currently at the perfect age. At 12, he's old enough to be left responsible for Phillip and Lilith, but young enough and naïve enough to fail to grasp why Stuart and I insist that he keeps them bathing for a full half-hour, with the door closed. We tell him that it's to "make sure they are totally clean", or "because they love their bath times, and it's unfair to stop them playing".

I'm stood on the landing in my lazy-day, faded dressing gown – Shiraz-coloured lingerie hidden underneath – with my arms crossed, ready to pound on Declan's door. Before I resort to that, though, I hear footsteps.

My sleepy-looking son Declan opens the entrance to his dim pit, swarmed by early-morning body odour. He yawns. Yellow sleep crusts his eyes beneath the darkness of his wild fringe. He's got a little caterpillar of bum-fluff on his upper lip, and the other day I heard his voice squeak for the first time. I'm starting to anticipate the teen angst that's no doubt to come, but for the moment he's paused at an adorably gawky stepping-stone between childhood and adolescence, like a crude and incomplete copy of his father.

"What time is it?" Declan asks.

"It's 10 o'clock, *sweetie*," I say, forcing the word. I'm keen for Stuart's hand on my hair again. It always feels awkward when I'm aroused but have to speak to the kids. "The twins need their 30 minutes in the bath, but you'll be happy to hear that the weather is good, so we *are* going to Castle Land."

Declan beams a dopey smile, no doubt considering Castle Land's gravity-defying rides. "Okay, cool."

I tell him, "Now get in there and start running the water. I'll bring up the terrors."

Declan shuffles past me to the bathroom. I head downstairs, following the sounds of laughter and tears, which in this house are generally inseparable. My husband still stands at the lounge window, looking out across our garden into our neighbour's front yard. Lilith has her arms hooked around Stuart's neck and is bawling dramatically, while my little survivor Phillip sits on the floor, hanging onto his daddy's feet, rocking and giggling.

"All under control here, then," I say, noticing the white, lumpy spray on Stuart's shoulder that Lilith had almost certainly coughed up.

"What?" Stuart asks calmly, over the sound of Lilith's whines. Even standing there, amidst the warzone of our twins' morning mischief, Stuart epitomises reassuring authority. "Ssshhhh, princess," he tells Lilith, and pecks her rosy cheek.

Lilith calms, which only means that my little survivor will start crying again soon, at which point Lilith will no doubt start laughing instead.

"Here," I say, offering to take Lilith. "My little puke-bag." I take her from Stuart, cradling her bottom and hugging her warmth to my chest. She chuckles, a wriggling parcel of kid-smells. Down on the floor, Phillip starts to snivel.

I hear Declan say, "Bath's running. Let's get this over with."

Declan pads into the lounge, scoops up Phillip from the carpet and then takes Lilith from me into his other arm. He's perfected the technique for holding the two toddlers simultaneously, aided no doubt by the fact that he has inherited his father's broad frame. The twins gaze at him in awe, one on either side, forgetting their habit of trading laughter for tears. Sometimes I think that they have more hero worship for their big brother than they have for their own dad, which makes me wonder if the two men of the house will clash at some point.

I had hoped that as soon as Declan had carried the twins upstairs I would see that look of achingly stern lust pass over Stuart's face, but instead my husband keeps staring through the window at next door's lawn.

"Haven't seen Mr Crisp," Stuart says. "I've been here for almost an hour, and he hasn't taken his morning walk."

Our cul-de-sac is empty and the sun has conjured a

golden veil over the morning.

From behind him I wrap my arms around his firm stomach and press my cheek to the back of his shoulder – the one without the baby puke. "You've been trying to spy on our kindly old next-door neighbour?"

Stuart grunts a laugh. "No. But he's usually like clockwork. Leaves the house at 10:30 to pick up his newspaper and whatever else he needs, and always back by 11. You think he's sick?"

"I don't know," I say, sliding a hand down to cup Stuart's balls. "But what I do know, is that we have a little spare mummy and daddy time…"

"Perhaps I should go round and make sure he's okay."

I squeeze Stuart gently through the fabric. He muffles a groan.

"I can think of a more interesting way to spend the next 30 minutes."

"Well, maybe if I…" His words become a gasp as I reach into his pyjama pants and rake my nails down the shaft of his thickening cock.

I tell him, "Can't you make sure that *I'm* okay first, and then maybe call round to see Mr Crisp?"

He whirls on me, and *there's* the expression I've been seeking. "You need to be reminded of one or two things, young lady."

I freeze as I feel his hand behind me, scaling my spine. It comes to rest amongst my tousled hair before wrenching it sideways, hard enough to make my eyes water. I keep my eyes defiantly open, though, and grip his wrist in one hand.

I say, "Maybe *you* need to be reminded of a couple of things, boy."

Stuart's lips twist as if he's suppressing laughter.

"Really?"

I take his balls in one hand and squeeze, not hard enough to hurt, but firm enough to carry the message. His body language softens and he releases my hair. I smile, trying to summon some confidence, and lead him by the wrist upstairs.

Jonathan Butcher

5. Girl

Daddy always says, "Don't be silly," when I ask him about other Girls and other places. He points around My Room and says, "This is what you get." Then he says, "I bring you food and films and books, and I keep you safe and I fuck you Good. A Good Girl should always say thank you to her Daddy, for keeping her safe."

And if I ever ask him a second time, My Daddy spanks my face and says, "See, that's what you get."

Now, I'm standing at the bottom of the stairs in front of My Room, outside for the first time ever. There is a long bright light high above me, and a door at the top of the stairs.

What if I get up to the door and open it, but there's just another wall? What if there is no "outside," and this is all there is – this, and my other Daddies who sometimes appear and disappear? Or, what if I open the door and there are just more doors that carry on and on and on, and never end?

I wonder if these steps will be as easy to climb as they are for the Daddies and the other Girls who sometimes climb them in the films. I lift one foot up and put it on the first stair. I push, and bring my other foot up too. It's easy, but I hold onto the long piece of wood at my side.

The stairs feel cold and hard under my feet. My chest keeps thumping and my head feels tight and I keep thinking that I'm going to puke.

I have a film where loads of Daddies stand around a Girl, pissing on her. While they piss, they say 1, 2, 3, 4, 5, 6, all the way up to 15. So, as I climb, I say 1, 2, 3, 4, 5, 6, and it makes it easier. I reach 15 but then I don't know what to say next, so I go back to 1 for the last few steps.

Everything gets darker when the stairs stop. Something feels warm and soft under my feet, like My Daddy's clothes. Is this … floor-clothes?

I look away from my feet and away from the floor-clothes and up to the door. I hold the handle and twist it and pull it open. There is just darkness inside. It smells different though. It smells Good.

I count 1, 2, 3, 4, 5, 6, up to 15, and then I step inside. The long light from above the stairs only brightens up this new room a little bit. I nearly start to cry, but instead I push against the wall on the other side. There is suddenly too much light, so I squeeze my eyes shut.

It isn't cold up here, and it smells like something that would taste Good in my mouth. I open my eyes, just a bit.

I'm standing somewhere that's bigger than My Room. There are two really, really bright square lights on one wall. I can't see much, but I think that I can see what smells Good. It's a small, brown circle that's sitting on what looks like a big flat shiny bed.

I want to eat it.

The brown circle has been cut open, and inside there is some darker brown stuff that looks like shit. I scrunch up a handful and when I eat it, I almost start to cry again. This round, brown circle tastes better than porridge and water and bread and cheese and My Daddy's cock, so I don't stop eating until it's all gone.

When I'm done, I don't feel as shaky as before. I still feel different, though, and my throat is all tight, as if there's a cock in it.

The bright lights don't seem so bright now. When I look around, there's some of the same stuff that I have seen in the films, and everything is square and bright and white and smooth and smells Good. I think about going back through the little dark room and down the stairs to My Room, and then maybe sitting down next to My Daddy to see if he wakes up. But I'm not going to.

I want to find another Good Girl.

In the corner, something big, shiny and square goes all the way up to the ceiling. The ceiling up here doesn't have any pipes, like the one in My Room, and next to the big shiny square thing there is a bright door made of screen.

I think that I want to go through it, but what if that's where my other Daddies are?

On the other wall, below the two big bright screens, there is something metal and deep and wet. There are two taps above it, just like the sink in my bathroom, but it can't be a sink because it's metal and looks too big.

Something shines in the light from the screens. It's a metal thing, and its shape makes me think of the bits of screen sticking out of My Daddy's face. I pick it up, but then I yelp and drop it when it touches the place on my hand that was cut by the piece of screen in My Daddy's face.

I take the long metal thing into my other hand and go to the door made of screen. This door doesn't have a handle like the one in My Room or like the one at the top of the stairs, but there is something small and round at the same height as my eyes.

I twist the small round thing and everything goes white.

6. Serenity

Stuart smiles almost sarcastically as he lies down naked on our bed. He looks huge, lying on his back with his head on the pillow and his feet reaching the end of the mattress. His erection teeters like a Jenga stack.

"Don't you fucking *dare* move," I tell him.

As much as I adore the feeling of being directed, *guided*, when we have sex, another part of me likes to resist the same roles every time. I swing a thigh over Stuart's face and kneel above him on the bed, my vulva an inch or so from his lips.

"Push out your tongue, boy," I whisper. If I speak any louder the kids might hear, even over the splashing, giggling and crying coming from the bathroom across the landing.

Stuart is expressionless as I slip and gyrate against his

tongue, raising myself up an inch to give him time to catch a breath before plunging back down and smothering his red face again. Even after giving birth to three kids, even after hearing me use the toilet through the bathroom door a thousand-and-one times, even after my breasts have started to droop and my stomach has attained a ruffled, post-pregnancy sag, Stuart *still* likes how I taste.

"Yeah, you love that slit, don't you?" I tell him, ignoring how awkward the words sound to me.

Stuart tries to nod but I have him clamped between my thighs. I can feel his arms tense as he struggles to keep them at his sides. I'm pushing his boundaries a little, and even feel tempted to press a wet fingertip between his buttocks. When I slide downwards again, sticky and wet, Stuart sucks my clitoris between his lips. His eyes meet mine and their gaze hardens. I hesitate. His tongue flicks the hood and he sucks harder. I'm tempted to pull away; too much stimulation there feels more irritating than arousing, but I don't want to surrender yet.

"You know what happens if you keep doing that, don't you, boy?" I say, but my voice has weakened.

I lift my hips but Stuart keeps his mouth encircling my clitoris. He's known to be a somewhat bratty submissive, but this is real disobedience as he draws the pink flesh further between his lips. If I'm not mistaken he even lets his teeth brush my labia. He knows how I hate that and I can feel my sexual authority waning, slipping back into our usual roles.

It feels more natural when Stuart is in control anyway, so with a touch of reluctance I pull back. My flesh slips from his mouth with a soft plop. Perched on his chest, staring down into his juice-soaked face, I try not to feel deflated.

His lips are a twitch away from that satisfied smile again.

"My turn, then," I say. "Cuff me and fuck me while we still have time."

"Cuffs?" he asks, but I know he wants to. He *loves* having me at his mercy.

I listen to the kids splashing and laughing in the bath, and again thank the world for Declan being such a trustworthy lad.

"We've got 10 minutes," I tell Stuart.

Jonathan Butcher

7. Girl

It's bright and warm outside. The air is moving and everything is really, REALLY big. There's green and blue and yellow and white and all the colours I've seen in films and in pictures, but it's not on a screen or in a magazine or in a book – it's all around me.

I want to scream.

I sit down onto some tickly green stuff and hold one hand over my mouth. I shuffle backwards on my nice tight ass until I'm backed up against a wall. It is lumpy and nothing like the red bricks in My Room. I put my head on my knees and squeeze the metal thing.

Even though I only said that I liked it and didn't really, I wish that My Daddy was fucking my nice smooth cunt in My Room. I wish that he was telling me that I'm a Good Girl, even though the things he does hurt. Like he always says, there's only "Good" and "different", but being outside like this is maybe *too different*.

I shut my eyes, thinking about the red stuff all over My Daddy's face. I think about the long metal thing in my hand and I think, maybe I should scratch the Bad away. Maybe I should make the red stuff come out of my belly or my face or my cunt, but then I get shaky again and think about my other Daddies, about putting the metal thing into them and the Daddies in my films, and even into My Daddy, too.

There are noises all around me, whistling and groaning and whispering and buzzing and sounds that might be cars, like the ones from the books and the Other Film. It's big and loud and REALLY DIFFERENT, but if I keep looking at the tickly green stuff on the floor I might not scream.

My mouth goes wet like a nice smooth cunt and I bring my head up off my knees. I puke. It goes down over my tits and my belly, yellow and stinky.

This room is too big and bright and I want to be somewhere small again.

I look up from the puke and from the tickly green stuff. There's a wall and a big green thing in front of me, and there are bugs on the ground like the ones I get in My Room sometimes, except bigger and with more colours. I look up past the big green thing and up past the wall. There's a really, really bright light above me where the ceiling should be, and even though it looks far away I think that it must be bigger than anything in My Room. I think it must be even bigger than 15 of my rooms, all put together, and a thought like that makes me want to puke again.

I keep holding the metal thing and get onto all fours and crawl with my ass pushed out, just like I do when Daddy fucks me from behind. Daddy always says, "Don't arch your back, push your ass out, Good Girl," so that's how I crawl. Then I think, no. I'm not going to get fucked today because My Daddy is asleep, so instead of pushing my ass out I just crawl, looking at the tickly green stuff and the metal thing in my hand, and not looking up at the big blue ceiling.

Something drops in front of me. It's the size of a hand or a cock. It's black and it has a long yellow nose, and it looks at me with its twitchy head. I almost scream, but then it jumps and disappears into the bright blue light above me.

I look back at the ground again and keep crawling, and then reach something wooden that looks like a wall or a door. I get up onto my knees and pull down the handle using the hand holding the metal thing. Nothing happens, but when I lift it up, it opens.

Behind the wall-door, there are more green things and more walls. Everything smells like piss. I crawl and my hand hurts from where I hit My Daddy's face. I turn my head and see that the walls go on, in front of me and behind me.

There are sleeping cars at one end, *real cars*, like in the Other Film, and there's something else, too.

There's a little Daddy.

Even though he's really little, I know he's a Daddy because he has short hair. I stop crawling and just look at him.

The little Daddy is sitting on the ground with his back to me. He has a yellow car in his hand, like the kind I saw in the Other Film. He moves the car across the ground, forwards and backwards, the same way that a cock moves when it's fucking. I still feel shaky but I don't feel too different right now, and I don't want to puke or sleep.

The little Daddy moves the car in a circle, following it round. He's got golden hair and a small nose. His white top-clothes say "YUM YUM DONUTS". He's sticking his tongue out. When he sees me, he smiles.

I get up onto my knees and the little Daddy looks at my tits and my cunt. He stops smiling. Suddenly, he screams like a Bad Girl in one of the films. I don't want any big Daddies to come, so I jump forwards and grab his face and press my hand over his mouth.

He keeps trying to scream, so I push the metal thing into his chest really, really hard.

The little Daddy coughs red stuff all over my fingers. He shakes his head and falls down, so I pull him backwards through the wooden wall-door and close it again. While he's lying on the tickly green stuff with his legs kicking and his arms squirming, I keep my hand over his lips and drag the metal thing out of his chest. He's not screaming now, but his mouth goes, "ACK, ACK, ACK."

I push the metal thing into his belly and pull it out really fast, in and out, in and out, like I'm fucking him. Soon, his white top-clothes are all red and he falls asleep with his eyes open, staring up and past me.

The little Daddy's legs are spread open, like a Good Girl waiting to be fucked. It makes me think about the little Daddy's cock. It can't be as big as My Daddy's, but will it get big one day?

I push the metal thing through his leg-clothes, into the place where his cock is. As I push it in and pull it out, I count 1, 2, 3, 4, 5, 6, up to 15.

"You like it when I do that, don't you?" I whisper, as I pull out the metal thing. "Because you're a Good Girl."

I think about checking to see if he has lost all of his cock, and maybe chewing on whatever's left, like I did with My Daddy, but then there is a very loud noise.

Past the walls of the big place where My Room is, there are other big green things. All of the ground is green and tickly and everything smells sweet, like soap, or like an apple. The loud noise comes again, and something that might be a really big car goes by.

I put a hand over my mouth. My palm tastes like red stuff.

I don't want to go back to My Room, but I don't want to stay here with the sleeping little Daddy, and I don't want to go back through the wooden wall-door, or go towards the place with the cars.

Behind the sleeping little Daddy there is a wooden wall. I crawl past the little Daddy and stand up and reach up to the top of the wooden wall. I jump, like I do when I'm doing my exercising. The wood feels prickly on my hands, just like my pubes feel when they start to grow back whenever I've been a Bad Girl and forgotten to shave them. I pull my head up above the wooden wall and there's another room without a ceiling, with more big green things and a green floor and some other little things that are coloured blue and red and yellow. There's also something small with four legs, black hair and big yellow eyes.

"Dog," I say, feeling dizzy.

When I pull my foot up and over the top of the wooden wall, the thing with four legs, the dog, disappears under one of the big green things. The wood feels sharp against my cunt so I pull my other foot over and drop down onto the tickly green stuff in the new room.

There is another big place here, with walls and two doors made of screen next to each other. It looks a lot like My Daddy's big place.

If my Daddy stays in the big place where My Room is, maybe there is another Daddy who stays in *this* one.

Maybe there is another Good Girl who always stays in Her Room, too.

When I walk over to the door made of screen I feel different again, but not too shaky. I pull down the handle and step inside.

8. Serenity

If only we had the whole day free. It used to happen sometimes before the twins were born, when Stuart had the day off from the office and when Declan was at school or with friends. We would spend hours in bed, exploring.

"Good slut," Stuart breathes, looking down at me as I lie on my back with my hands cuffed to opposite bedposts. My ass will probably bruise from his bites, because we can't spank or do anything too loud with the kids in the house. Stuart says, "You don't deserve to see me, do you?"

"No, sir," I reply, glancing at the clock before he blindfolds me. Still five minutes before there's any risk of the kids' bath time ending.

Stuart covers my eyes with a black leather mask and slips between my legs to lick me, but more roughly than when we make love. He bites my thighs and slaps my clit,

35

pinches my buttocks and pushes his tongue into my ass. I have to clench my teeth to stop crying out.

I cum quickly, silently, and my head becomes muzzy. As my inner muscles tighten around Stuart's fingers I hear him coo.

"That's nice," he says. "What a good little slut you are."

Somewhere beyond my submissive roleplay my mind fills with love for the father of my children. He's the Big Spoon to my Little Spoon, the friend and partner who informs me when he thinks I'm right or wrong, and tells me that I'm beautiful, even though I'm not as young or as firm as I once was.

I feel Stuart clamber up the bed, his thighs on either side of me. The heavy bob of his erection climbs a trail between my breasts.

"Wait," I hiss.

My eye-mask has turned the room black and featureless, but I can still hear the kids splashing in the tub.

Behind the bathroom door, Declan says, "Lilith, stop trying to eat Phil's boat."

I thought I'd heard something else, though.

Stuart halts his path towards my mouth, no doubt listening too.

From the bathroom there's the unmistakable noise of Lilith's tears, Phillip's chuckles and Declan muttering, "Goddamn it."

"It's okay," Stuart says, his voice firm and reassuring as he continues his climb.

I feel his hand grasp my throat. Something about the movement of the air and the positioning of his weight tells me that his other hand is leaning against the wall behind me. I smell him more strongly as the head of his cock prods my chin.

I stretch open my mouth and lie obediently still as he glides his erection between my lips, moving it along my tongue towards the back of my mouth where it presses against my well-trained gag reflex. I can tell that Stuart is at his stiffest by how thick his veins feel, bulging against my upper lip.

"You beautiful … fucking whore …" he gasps, and thrusts between my lips, continuing to grip my throat. "You want it so bad, don't you?"

"Yes sir," I say, but because my mouth is filled and my throat is closed, my affirmation sounds more like panicked denial.

Beneath the noise of his panting and my own heartbeat thumping in my temples, I hear a sound like rushing footsteps.

Stuart's breathing halts. He freezes.

The head of Stuart's cock remains between my lips, motionless, as though he's delaying his orgasm. There's no time though. I'm about to urge him on, to remind him that the kids will be out of the bathroom and needing to be dressed for Castle Land soon, when warm fluid coats my chin.

"Mmm, thank you sir," I say, stretching out my tongue to catch the semen.

The liquid isn't coming from the end of Stuart's cock, though, and it tastes different.

I hear a high-pitched whimper.

"Stuart?" I ask.

He breathes a single word – "*What?*" – before his weight topples sideways.

"Stuart? *Stuart?*"

Wrapped in the leather mask's artificial darkness, I become aware of a third presence.

A voice that I've never heard before, female and gristly and low, says: "Yes, that's right. Show me that tight asshole."

9. Girl

"Who is that?" the Girl on the bed says.

I wriggle the metal thing, tugging it a bit.

The Daddy goes, "UH."

The metal thing slides out of his tight asshole. It goes, SHLUP.

"Please," the Girl says. "Who is that? What have you done?"

This big place is even warmer and even bigger than My Daddy's big place.

I had walked in and heard noises from up some stairs. At the top, behind a white door, I had seen a Daddy fucking a Girl's mouth on a bed. Seeing it had made me think of when My Daddy had fucked my mouth and made me puke. That had made me feel shaky and even more different, and I'd thought, *It should be them, not us*. So I had held the metal thing out front of me, stepped forwards really fast, and shoved it up the Daddy's ass.

The Daddy hasn't looked at me. He's lying on the bed with his ass up, which is dribbling red stuff. He's half-on top of the Girl and he's breathing different and holding his balls where the metal thing had come out. He's biting his lip and his eyes are all white.

"Hello? Who are you?" the Girl on the bed says.

She can't see me because she has a black thing covering her eyes. She's panting really quickly, going "HUH HUH HUH HUH HUH."

I pull the Daddy off her. He groans, like he's cumming, and his eyes stop being white. He looks at me with his mouth hanging open and says, in a whispery voice, "It's a girl."

Maybe I should make him fall asleep and turn him into a Good Girl, like I did to the little Daddy on the tickly green stuff. He kicks his legs out, like he's trying to stand up, but then he goes, "HEEEEE," and stops moving.

I feel really, *really* different when I look at the Girl on the bed. I don't think I've ever seen a real Girl before. She is still gasping. She has short, messy brown hair that makes her look really cute, and she has tits and a cunt like I do and like they do in the films, but she's … *here*.

I step forwards. She squeaks like she's being spanked.

"What are you doing?" she asks, and her voice is really scratchy. She curls her legs up to get away from me but she can't move her arms because they're spread wide, with her left wrist and her right wrist handcuffed to the opposite bedposts.

A voice from behind me goes, "Dad! Can you come get the twins? I'm going to shower now!"

The Daddy on the bed looks towards the door. "Declan…" he says, but it's like he can't breathe.

"Declan!" the Girl on the bed shouts. "Take the twins and run! Get out of here!"

The Daddy on the bed looks at me. Then he looks at the door. Then he looks at the Girl on the bed.

"Stay still," I tell him.

I hear something click, and when I turn, I see a littler Daddy standing in the doorway.

"Declan," I say, repeating what the Daddy on the bed and the Girl had called him.

When Declan sees me, he looks like he gets smaller. Behind him, there are two shapes sitting in a big white thing filled with water. I can't see if they are Daddies or Girls.

"Declan," I say again.

Declan's mouth opens and closes and opens again.

"Here," I say to Declan. I click my fingers and point to the floor next to me, just like I saw a Daddy do in a film. That Daddy's Girl had a ballgag and a buttplug and nipple clamps that had pinched her tits. She was crying, but she had done as the Daddy had told her.

Declan just stands there though, like a Bad Girl.

"Declan!" the Girl on the bed shouts. "If you can't run, stay in the bathroom and lock the door!"

Declan nods really fast and steps backwards. He shuts the other door with a click so I turn back to the Girl on the bed.

The Daddy is groaning again, but not like Daddies do when they get cocksucked. He groans like Girls do when their Daddies hit them or burn them or make them feel shaky and different. He looks at the Girl on the bed and takes one red hand off his balls, and then reaches up and pulls the black thing down off the Girl's eyes.

Jonathan Butcher

10. Serenity

I've only ever seen this look on Stuart's face once before; when we thought that Phillip, my little survivor, was going to live no more than an hour after his birth. Stuart's look is a childlike gaze of disbelief and pleading, as if for a few frozen moments I'm no longer his lover, but his mother. I see him half-sprawled beside my naked legs, gazing up at me. I see him gripping his crotch. I see the fan of blood that has sprayed across the sheets and over my breasts.

I *taste* that blood.

The shape of our intruder fills my peripheral vision, but at first I am too afraid to look. When I break eye contact with my husband and take in her sight at last, I do so with both revulsion and unexpected pity.

A thin, late-adolescent girl with an underbite stands nude at the foot of our bed, gripping a long Japanese-style chef's knife at her side, its point slicked red. Her dark brown hair reaches her waist, unstyled but clean, reminding me of a schoolchild's despite the fact that she is almost a woman. A mess of fresh and fading bruises mark her upper arms, and her wrists are tracked with what appear to be scratch marks, some of which have scabbed. She takes me in with dull, grey eyes that are never still. Below them, her lips are streaked red and her small breasts speckled with what could be vomit.

My first impression is that the girl does not appear angry, or frenzied, or delirious; above all things, she appears disoriented.

With my arms still cuffed to the bed and my husband so clearly injured, I have never felt so helpless.

"What did you do?" I ask, as the world feels as though it is dropping away beneath me.

The girl blinks. A tremor crosses her face. "Daddies shouldn't fuck girls like they do. The other film said."

Behind her, across the landing, the bathroom door cracks open and Declan peers out, eyes wet with tears.

I shout, "Declan, lock that door again, *now!*"

The girl turns, snarling suddenly, and using both hands she raises the knife over her head like a sword. Declan sucks in air and yanks the door shut. I hear him fumble with the lock.

The girl looks back at me, her face losing its animation and falling blank. "What happens after they go to sleep?"

Stuart groans.

"Quiet," she tells him.

I struggle to see past my husband's agony. "After who go to sleep?"

"When the red stuff comes out, like your daddy, when

do they wake up?"

My insides twist at her words but I summon an icy stillness, the kind with which I responded to my husband's terror, just over a year ago. We had held each other on that hospital bed, facing the likelihood that our newborn son would die before we had even named him. Stuart had looked at me, as if in search of answers that I did not possess. My little survivor Phillip pulled through though, so now, staring back at my husband, I decide that Phillip will be my focus: I will remember that he lived on, despite all signs having pointed towards his death. If Phillip could survive that, then my family can survive anything.

"This isn't my daddy," I tell the girl, nodding at Stuart. "This is my husband. And if he falls asleep after you have hurt him like this, he might not wake up. He…" – I choke back a sob – "He might die."

The girl speaks as though she is dreaming. "My daddy might not wake up, then."

"Did you…" I begin, trying not to let panic melt away my calm, wanting to keep her talking. "Did you hurt someone else, too?"

Stuart moans again and I feel his body tense beside me. I've had no medical training and can't imagine the pain of what I assume must be his stab wound. I glance at his exposed backside, and despite my rising horror feel dimly relieved that his blood is not rushing out at an alarming rate.

Our intruder says, "I hurt my Daddy because he caught me being a bad girl." Her hands are shaking. "I was watching the other film and he didn't like it. He turned it off, and then I got shaky and felt different and I pushed him and hit him with the screen and then he fell asleep."

She bites her lower lip like a disobedient child, and her eyes flit across the bed and then down across her own body. One of her hands leaves the knife and rakes her other arm with its short, sharp nails.

"One, two, three…" she counts, but then stops as a realisation alters her face. She looks at the blade and raises it to her drawn stomach.

"No, no…" I say.

The girl drags the knife through the flesh from her navel around to her side, mewling like an injured animal.

"No, *honey*, no."

The term of endearment leaves my mouth unbidden, and seems to break even Stuart's agonised concentration. He looks up, face pained but quizzical.

The unexpected word alerts me to something.

This girl may have assaulted my husband, who now lies bleeding and on the brink of unconsciousness beside me. She may have forced my children to hide themselves in a locked room, shielded by nothing but a flimsy wooden door. She may have rendered me helpless and terrified for my family's life – *but she too needs protection.*

I have seen milder forms of her behaviour in friends, in "problem children" at Declan's school, and even once in an old lover. I know as surely as I know my own name that this girl has suffered trauma, abuse; it glares out from her bruises, scratches and scars, from her childish phrasing and her trembling body language.

As I watch the girl carve trickling divots into her stomach, I realise something with unimpeded clarity: my little survivor Phillip may very well have escaped death when he was born, but that was then, and this is now.

The truth is, this girl could very well kill us all.

11. Girl

The metal thing is very Good at scratching the Bad away, and as I close my eyes and scratch my stomach, I almost feel like I'm back in My Room again.

The Girl on the bed is saying something.

"Honey, no. No."

She sounds like a girl from one of the films, a girl who says, "No no no," to a Daddy, but whose Daddy keeps saying, "Yes yes yes."

I open my eyes.

The Daddy on the bed says, "Uh." He sounds sleepy and his ass is still drooling red stuff. I feel like a Bad Girl, but the Daddy shouldn't have been fucking the Girl's mouth because Daddies shouldn't fuck Girls like they do – the Other Film said so.

I get shaky again, but I've scratched the Bad away for now. My belly hurts much worse than when I use my nails or when I hit my arms against the wall. Worse, so it's better.

"What's your name?" the Girl on the bed asks. She has really big eyes, and her tits shudder when she breathes. Even though she is naked and her arms are outstretched and handcuffed, she doesn't look much like a Girl from one of the films. Those Girls are little, thinner, and their skin is smoother and their tits rounder.

"What's your name?" she asks me again.

The Daddies and the Girls in my books have names like Kate or Lolita or Sally, but My Daddy says that I am too Good to have a name. My Daddy says that I am so Good that he has to keep me safe in My Room.

I don't say anything to the Girl on the bed, because I don't know what to say.

"What do you want?" she asks me.

I just say, "Daddies shouldn't fuck Girls like they do."

The Girl on the bed's face changes. She has her Daddy's red stuff all over her chin. "Look…I want to help you," she says. "There are other people who will want to help you, too. But I can't do anything while I'm stuck here. If you unlock these…" She rattles the handcuffs. "…I will try to help. I promise. Just…please let me call the hospital for Stuart, here."

She's saying words that I don't know. It makes my head fill with voices and colours and cocks splitting cunts and assholes open and I hear myself say, "Urrrrrgggghhh," but that doesn't help, so I use the metal thing to scratch some more of the Bad away, scratching it over my tits and my shoulders and my belly.

The Girl on the bed says, "No no no no no."

Even though she doesn't stop me using the metal thing,

I notice that it isn't scratching the Bad away anymore. Everything is so different and I keep thinking of Daddies fucking me and words that I don't understand and all the red stuff I've seen today.

"Stop!" the Girl says.

I stop, but the voices and the pictures keep coming.

What if I scratch the Daddy's Bad away, instead of mine?

I hurry to the other side of the bed. The Girl shuts up like a Good Girl and watches me watching her Daddy. I crouch down and look at his sleepy face, with its eyes closed and its whistling breath.

The Girl shakes her handcuffs against the bed, and yells, "Stop! Don't!"

The red stuff coming from the Daddy's ass has slowed down. I'm thinking about the Other Film, and about the films with the Daddies fucking the Girls, and about my Daddy fucking me, and about this Daddy fucking the mouth of the Girl on the bed.

They shouldn't fuck us like they do.

The Girl on the bed says, "Please please please, don't!"

I hold the metal thing up as I look down at the Daddy's face. His cheek is flat against the bed. I take hold of his hair and point the metal thing down at him.

The Girl is still saying, "Please please please."

I remember one of the films, and for a second I feel Good.

"Yeah that's it," I tell the Girl's Daddy. "I wanna see you puke."

So I put the end of the metal thing against his lips, as if it was a big thick cock, and I push. His eyes don't open, but the metal thing slides into his mouth sideways. It

49

scrapes on his teeth: CCRRTTCCCTRRRTTTCCCK.

The Girl rattles her handcuffs and kicks her legs. "Wake up, Stuart! Do something!"

When I have slid half of the metal thing into the Daddy's mouth, his eyes open a little. I hold onto his hair, though, really tight. He looks sleepy, like My Daddy sometimes does after he's been fucking me for a long time.

This Daddy's eyes go really big when I shove the metal thing further into his mouth. He makes a noise like a little Girl cocksucking a Daddy, and when I pull the metal thing back out, one side of his lips and face opens up, red-and-pink like a nice spread cunt. I let go of the Daddy's hair. He splutters and red stuff comes out of his lips and down his cheek.

"You fucking *bitch*!" the Girl on the bed screeches.

The Daddy coughs again. It sounds wet. He looks confused. A spurt of orange stuff runs down his chin, and then he coughs some more and a big load of red stuff shoots out of his mouth and goes all over the bedsheets.

The Girl says "Stuart! Look at me, Stuart!"

There's a noise. I turn around. The little Daddy called Declan is looking out at me from behind a door. I rush at him. The door shuts but I keep going and slam my shoulder against the wood.

BAM.

I hit the door with the back of the metal thing really, really fast.

BAM BAM BAM BAM BAM.

A little voice behind the door calls, "Mum!"

Behind me, the Girl on the bed says, "Please stop!"

I bang and bang and bang with the metal thing, but the door won't open.

I look back at the Girl on the bed and at the Daddy who I made puke, the one who she had called Stuart. He's still coughing and it sounds all spitty, and the red stuff and the orange puke keeps slopping down his face and over the sheets. He has one hand on his cock and one hand on his throat, and he's shivering, like a Girl who has been spanked until she cums.

The Girl is crying. She's still saying "Please stop," but more quietly now.

"Ssshhh, don't cry," I tell her, like My Daddy sometimes says after my other Daddies come to see me.

I go back to the bed and stroke the Girl's hair. She whimpers and looks down at her tits.

Maybe I should try and scratch *her* Bad away, too. Then maybe the little Daddy called Declan will come out from behind the other door and I will make *his* red stuff come out too. Maybe if I do these things, I will feel less shaky and different, because that way, everyone else will be asleep.

I lift the metal thing and hold the sharp point against the Girl's chin. I start crying and she looks up at me. At least she's stopped kicking and doesn't tell me to stop.

I think I know what I have to do, so I hold her by the back of her hair, pull up her chin, and move the metal thing down to her throat.

Jonathan Butcher

12. Serenity

"You're right," I tell the girl, when she presses the knife point against my neck. "Daddies shouldn't fuck us like that."

The words are part last resort, part appeal for empathy. The girl's eyes look intoxicated, as if she's approaching the end of a heavy drinking binge, but through the bloodshed and through all that I imagine she has suffered, *she hears me.*

I know with my guts that whenever she says, "daddy", she means "men". This is a girl, a *child*, who either has severe learning difficulties, or is addled by drugs, or has been so diminished by her experiences that she can no longer function healthily, if she ever could – but when I agree with her, her eyes flutter in recognition.

"My daddy won't fuck me anymore. I made him go to sleep," she says. She releases a little of the knife's pressure on my neck. "We could make your daddy go to sleep, too."

I ignore the obscene suggestion and concentrate on her lips and her crushed body language. I stare at these things because all that I truly want to do is tear off these fucking handcuffs and annihilate her before calling an ambulance for Stuart, whose spluttering and drifting consciousness (for all I know) signals imminent death. He has bled so much already, soaking the bedsheets and his chest and thighs, but I mustn't dwell on his suffering or the risk this girl poses to us all.

"I bit my daddy's cock and I ate some of it, because that's what they did in the other film."

I ask, "Where is your room?"

"In the big place next to your big place. Through a really small room and down some stairs."

Stuart coughs. His pale face is pressed against a tacky pool of blood and vomit. His eyes are closed and his body is motionless, aside from his shivering. If he isn't dying, he's slipping into shock.

We were supposed to go to Castle Land...

"Do you like it when your daddy fucks you?" the girl asks.

I brace myself against an upsurge of sorrow, and tell her, "This is Stuart. He's not my daddy. We're married and he's my husband." I pause. "Do you know what that means?"

"Stuart," the girl says, seeming to test the word before shaking her head in reply. There's another subtle change in the knife's pressure.

"It means that Stuart and I want to be together. We love each other. We..."

I almost mention the children.

"…don't hurt each other."

"He was fucking you. He was hurting you."

Jesus Christ. She thinks she was helping.

"That was…a game," I say, trying to shape something complex into a concept that a child could understand. "Sometimes, people who are married play games. And these games can look bad, and they can look scary, but they're not."

"My daddy played games with me…"

"That's different," I insist. "Whatever has happened to you is not the same as the things that Stuart and I do."

The girl takes the knife away from my throat at last. With this movement the smell of her vomit mingles with a faecal scent seeping from Stuart's wound. She lowers the blade and settles her naked rump onto the mattress beside my legs.

"I thought that my daddy and my other daddies were…like Stuart," she says, angling her head as she looks at me. "I let them fuck my nice smooth cunt and my tight ass and my mouth."

I nod, relieved that she no longer has the blade against my skin.

She continues, "But the other film had two girls in it, and cars, and little daddies, and a dog, and a metal thing that sprayed fire. The girls said that they didn't like it when their daddies fucked them. And they said that girls should only like other girls."

I nod again. She moves closer, sliding her buttocks along the bed and looking at me, as though seeing me for the first time.

"Girls should only like other girls," she says again, and

leans down so that a wave of dark hair falls from her shoulder and strokes my right breast.

When she lowers her face towards mine, the scent of her yellow bile almost stings my nose. I strain against the handcuffs, wishing to either escape or at least transform the gesture into something affectionate, something kind and pure. Her bitter-tasting mouth presses to mine and my stomach lurches.

I'm reminded of the way my grandmother's dying breaths had tasted, before her gnarled hands had tightened to fists and then loosened as the life escaped her.

The teenager's tongue seeks the opening to my lips, and I summon the strength to thrust my head beyond her searching mouth and touch my cheek against hers. I'm struck by the idea of biting her throat, tearing away a bleeding chunk, but I'm too certain that no matter what horrors she has committed, even to those I love and adore, she is at present a *victim*, above all things. Despite the rational drive to tear into our aggressor's flesh and inflict a wound that will force her either to flee or protect herself, I can't. Instead, I kiss her blood-smeared cheek, partly because a dim, distant side of me thinks that she could be right.

Perhaps daddies – men – *shouldn't* do the things they do. I've had male strangers, partners, friends, and even family members touch me without my consent. Then there's the unwarranted blasting of car horns, the "accidental" brushing of hands against my ass or crotch at a busy concert, and the frequent expectation that if I show the slightest interest in a man it means that I'm flirting, it means that I *want him*.

As I press my lips to the girl's cheek, a half-buried

memory re-emerges.

When I was 9, my Uncle Ron flashed me. I was sat upon his bouncing knee, when all of a sudden there was an unzipping sound. I turned around and there it was, held between the trusted, stubby fingers of a hand that until then had only touched me in innocent ways. His penis reminded me of a mole on a nature programme – pink and curious. His breathing became shallow and he almost immediately withdrew his weapon, shoving it back into the darkness of his trousers.

I had never told anyone of the incident, not even Stuart, but my experience with once-sweet Uncle Ron means that every time I hear of a woman being mistreated, abused, assaulted, or raped, it echoes with one certainty: *that could have been me.*

So instead of attacking this bloody, violent girl, I swallow my terrors and try to comfort her. Buried beneath her hair, I ignore the stench of her stomach acids and peck her face repeatedly, pressing my mouth to her gummy skin without lust or longing, seeking only a connection, and a route to my family's survival.

"Sssshhh," I tell her. "Everything will be okay."

The girl freezes long enough for me to wonder if such intimacy will provoke the thrust of her blade.

"Am I a bad girl?" she asks, still leaning over me.

Torn, I whisper, "You just need some help. Now, if you let me out of these handcuffs, I can…"

The blow comes from nowhere.

Jonathan Butcher

13. Girl

When my head breaks, it's like the time when one of my other Daddies broke my head while he was fucking me from behind. He had said, "Ah that's nice, do that with your cunt again." Everything had gone black, and then he had broken my head again and said, "Ah that's nice."

Someone starts pulling my feet away, but all I can think is that I wish I was still hugging the Girl on the bed. Holding her had felt different to when My Daddy hugs me to stop me crying. It had felt ... warmer.

As I'm dragged down the bed, I hear the Girl say, "Oh God!"

I hit the floor. My nose goes CRUK, like the sound in the film when two Daddies keep punching a Girl tied to a chair.

Someone big presses onto my back. Air rushes out of my mouth.

"Declan, take the knife!" the Girl on the bed shouts.

I open my eyes. I'm looking at the floor-clothes, close up. I go stiff because the weight on my back makes me feel like I'm being fucked. That's what I do when I'm getting fucked sometimes, I go stiff, even when a Daddy says, "Shit, it's like fucking a corpse."

The bed above me rocks. Whoever is on my back shifts and I can breathe again. I twist my neck until it hurts. The little Daddy from the bathroom, Declan, is sitting on me, looking very shaky and very different. I want to cut his cock to pieces, but I also want to kiss his face like the Girl on the bed had kissed mine, and tell him, "Sssshhh, everything will be okay."

I hear a bump. I can't move, so I rest my face sideways against the floor-clothes. Two legs appear and, between them, a cock covered in red stuff.

"Hold her wrists," says Stuart, the Daddy who I'd fucked with the metal thing.

I remember the metal thing, but when I squeeze my fingers it's not there anymore.

Someone grabs both my arms and pulls them behind me. My shoulders go GLUCK and I feel the back of my hands touch each other. I can feel Declan's ass against my ass. I wait for him to put his cock inside me because I know they're going to fuck me. Then they're going to take me back to My Room where I will wait for my other Daddies. Then they'll *really* show me that I've been a Bad Girl.

"Stop moving," Stuart says. His voice scrapes like a cough. "Is she fighting?"

"No."

With my face sideways, I see the Daddy called Stuart

bend down. His hair is really short and his face is really white, but his eyes are big and staring and different, like he wants to fuck me and break my head and make me go to sleep, all at the same time.

Stuart leans towards me, closes his eyes and says "Ah." Red stuff patters on the floor. When Stuart disappears behind me, someone else pushes my arms against my back.

One weight leaves and something even heavier presses me down.

Stuart says, "Go to the dresser, get the key, and get those handcuffs off your mother."

"But-"

"*Do as your told.*"

They've swapped positions but Stuart isn't sitting on me, he's lying on me. I can feel his wet cock between my legs. It's soft, but sometimes my other Daddies' cocks stay soft when they want to fuck me, too.

"Be careful," I hear the Girl on the bed say.

Declan appears at my side, holding a shiny white board. It looks heavy.

Behind me, Stuart sounds sleepy when he says, "She isn't going anywhere."

Declan drops the white thing with a THUNG sound. He doesn't move and just watches me with his really big eyes.

"Don't hurt her," the Girl on the bed says.

"Don't … *don't hurt her?*" Stuart says, breathing hard through his nose. Something shoves my arms again, and Stuart says to me, "You'd deserve it, though, wouldn't you?"

"Declan, give me those," the Girl on the bed says. Something rattles. "Then give your father these and go check on the twins."

When Stuart's soft wet cock touches my cunt, he says quietly, "Ah."

Declan still stands there staring because he wants to fuck me, just like all the other Daddies. Even though I've cocksucked and been fucked lots and lots of times before, thinking about it happening again today makes me feel more different than ever.

"Give me the keys and go back to the bathroom, Declan," I hear the Girl on the bed tell him. She sounds urgent because Declan is still staring at me, not moving.

"Do as you're told, for Christ's sake!" Stuart shouts.

It's as if Declan is asleep, but with his eyes open really wide.

I think of the Girl on the bed kissing my face, and about how much I want to feel it again, and I take my chance: I push my ass back really, REALLY hard against Stuart's wet cock.

14. Serenity

Stuart wails and releases her wrists to protect his injured genitals. Declan stumbles backwards with a cry, snapped from his trance.

"Get me the fucking *keys*, Declan!" I yell.

Stuart's expression becomes hateful, and as the girl wriggles beneath him he slams a fist into the back of her skull. Her eyes swim, and for an instant I despise my husband for his brutality. The girl thuds face-first into the floor. Stuart grabs a handful of her hair and presses her face into the carpet. He grunts as she thrashes and bucks beneath him, but he holds her there.

Although Declan had struck the girl with the toilet lid while she and I had embraced, the blow does not seem to have slowed her. Declan leaves the lid lying where it is and reaches, not for the keys to my handcuffs, but for the girl's fumbled knife instead. He lifts it in one limp hand, like a child holding a toy, and it shimmers in the light from our window.

Helpless, I gaze on as my son points the knife at her.

While my husband struggles to keep her against the floor, his blood-smeared penis jostles against her naked rear.

"Help me, son!" he shouts, grabbing one of the girl's arms as her other flails and claws at the ground.

The girl ploughs backwards into his crotch again. Stuart grits his teeth, moaning, and when she bucks her tailbone once more he finally releases her to protect his wound.

The girl takes her opportunity: she swings one arm backwards and smashes her knuckles into Stuart's cheek. Stuart topples onto his side, his eyes wide.

The girl, lean and agile, rises to her knees and faces Declan. Her eyes are level with the blade as he jabs it towards her. The knife catches her cheek, draws blood, but with a sharp twist of her neck she sinks her teeth into Declan's wrist. He drops the blade, howling, and in one smooth movement the girl releases Declan and scoops the weapon up from the carpet. My son backs away, nursing his arm, and the girl remains on her knees, gripping the knife with her arm crooked, poised to strike.

"Honey," I say to her. "Please stop."

Declan becomes a statue against the wall, clutching his gnawed wrist. He no longer looks like a young man entering adolescence; now, he is very much a vulnerable little kid.

"What do you want?" I ask, hating the tremor in my voice.

The girl's lips part, perhaps to answer. Behind her,

Stuart's eyes have been drawn to the blade. As he rises silently to a partial sitting position, the girl closes her lips and spins on him.

She throws all of her weight into the blow. The knife blade vanishes like a magic trick, her hand and the plastic black handle halting only when they are flush against my husband's throat. A dark rose erupts from his gullet, and red vines burst from his lips to course down his chin. The girl wrenches the handle away and the blade reappears, now crimson. Somehow Stuart continues to lean on one arm, staring at her, remaining almost upright as the girl pulls herself to her feet. Stuart's expression is grim but he maintains his gaze, even as the blood pumps gurgling from his neck to run down his torso.

The girl lays her bare foot against my husband's chest and sends him sprawling backwards. He lands heavily, rotates once, and stops moving with his back to the bed.

I'm suddenly alone.

Cowardice weakens me. I want to sleep, or faint, or die. Then some primal urge thunders through me and I tear at the handcuffs still binding my wrists, screaming wordlessly. Through my rage I see the girl turn to Declan, who still has his back pressed to the wall, his eyes pooled with tears yet to run.

"*He's just a child!*" I shriek. "*For God's sake stop!*"

She does not seem to hear.

Through the cracked-open bathroom doorway I notice my little survivor Phillip standing upright, his blonde crown and piercing black eyes peeking over the edge of the tub.

"You want to fuck my nice smooth cunt," the girl says to Declan, the knife and her hand slick with my husband's blood. "Sssshhh, everything will be okay."

She ducks low. My son's tears finally trickle down his cheeks when she buries the knife between his legs and thrusts, thrusts, thrusts.

"One, two, three, four," she counts, as Declan buckles and slumps over her shoulder. "Five, six, seven…"

I can't hear her voice through my own screams but she maintains the assault for what feels like minutes. Declan's head judders with each knife thrust, his gaze pointed mournfully towards me. Then his streaming eyes lose focus.

In the silence afterwards, the girl lowers him gently to the ground, laying him onto his back like an adoring parent.

"Please," I say, no longer sure what I'm pleading for. "Please."

The girl looks gormlessly up from my son's corpse. "Even *little* Daddies want to fuck us."

15. Girl

The Girl on the bed is quiet now, even though her breathing is going, HUH HUH HUH. I really want to hug her again and say, "Sssshhh, everything will be okay," but I don't think she wants me to.

The little ones in the other room are quiet, now. I realise that I don't know if they are Girls or Daddies, so I get to my feet.

The floor, the Daddy named Stuart and the little Daddy named Declan are all covered in pools and pools of red stuff. I step over Stuart, holding the metal thing tightly just in case he wakes up and tries to fuck me again.

The Girl on the bed says, "Please," but her voice is like the little Girl in the film where the Daddy keeps fucking her with bigger and bigger buzzing toys. That little Girl had kept saying "Please please please," but the Daddy didn't listen. He kept fucking her until her cunt was really,

REALLY big, and the little Girl's voice was more like breathing than speaking.

One of the little ones from the other room looks up at me from a big white thing filled with water. This one is standing up, with hands on the edges of the white thing. The other one is sat down, with shoulders poking above the water. The one standing up is crying quietly and the one sitting down is smiling, but looks sad. They both have the same face.

"Please," the Girl on the bed says, a bit louder. I look back. She is looking at the Daddies on the floor. "Please. Please stop."

The little one standing up in the water in the other room has really big, dark eyes.

"Are you a Daddy or a Girl?" I ask it.

"They're *CHILDREN!!*" the Girl on the bed screams.

I put the metal thing down onto the toilet lid and pick up the standing little one. He has a really small cock, but he is definitely a Daddy. His face screws up and he shrieks into my ear, so I put him back in the water. The other little one starts to cry too, and in a little squeaky voice she screams, "Mummy!"

When I lift her up I see her little cunt. She wriggles in my hands as I put her back down into the water.

The Girl on the bed rattles the handcuffs against the wall. When she shouts, her voice has become strong again. "I'll do anything. If you stop, if you don't hurt them, I will do *anything* for you. What do you want? For God's sake, *tell me what you want!*"

I pick the metal thing up from the toilet lid. It's really, really red, just like my hands and my arms and the sleeping Daddies and the floor-clothes in the other room.

Maybe I should turn this little Daddy in the bathroom into a Good Girl, too. I hold the metal thing towards him. He reaches out with one fat hand.

"Please," the Girl on the bed says again.

The little Daddy wraps his fingers around the metal thing, and his dark eyes get even bigger. He pulls his hand back and it is covered in red stuff. He sees his fingers and giggles. The little Girl stands up to see. The little Daddy turns and strokes red stuff across her face. He laughs again. The little Girl looks like she's going to cry, but she just stares at me with her big dark eyes and the splat of her Daddy's red stuff on one cheek. She looks surprised. I laugh. She's a Good Girl.

The Girl on the bed screams and screams and suddenly the little Girl and the little Daddy start to cry together. I'm looking at the metal thing in my hand and thinking that maybe I should just make all of them fall asleep, but then I think, no, it should only be the Daddies.

I go back to the Girl on the bed. She's still screaming. Her eyes are shut and her handcuffed arms look shaky and her legs are closed, as if she doesn't want me to see her cunt.

Hysterical.

That's what My Daddy once said to me, the time that Red Daddy left my cunt covered in red stuff and I wouldn't stop crying. My Daddy said, "Stop being hysterical. Stop it, stop it."

"Stop being hysterical," I tell the Girl on the bed. "Stop it, stop it."

The Girl goes quiet. Her wet eyes make me think of broken screens.

"Please," the Girl says. "I'm their mother, for God's

sake."

Mother.

That word again. It makes me think of the hug that she had given me, and how she had kissed my cheek. That hug felt like the warmest place I've ever been.

"It's better if all the Daddies go to sleep, and don't wake up," I tell her. I want her to understand.

The Girl is still looking at the two Daddies on the floor. When she speaks, her voice is so quiet that I can hardly hear her: "*Yes.*"

"You're saying yes, but you mean no," I say. "You're like the Daddy in the film where the Girl says, 'Stop hitting me', and the Daddy says, 'Yes', but then he doesn't stop hitting her. He hits her more."

The Daddy in the bathroom gurgles.

The little Girl in the bathroom says, "*Urrrrrr.*"

The Girl on the bed *still* doesn't look up from the sleeping Daddies.

If I could show her that Daddies shouldn't *ever* fuck us like they do, that all the Daddies I've met are all the same, then maybe she'll understand.

Maybe she'll hug me again.

Maybe she'll even be my Mother.

16. Serenity

Without Stuart and Declan, death feels like a better option than survival.

The girl, blood-smeared and nude, remains vacant, watching me.

"I have to show you," she says. "I'll teach you."

Through the bedroom door, across the hall and into the next room, Phillip and Lilith stand side by side in the bathtub. Their dark eyes glitter, their mouths are slack, and their tiny hands grip the porcelain rim like birds' feet. For once, neither is crying and neither is laughing. Selfishly, detestably, I hope that if we are all to die, I am the first to be killed.

"I'll show you what daddies are really like," the girl says. She has been holding the knife limply in one hand, but when she raises it, blade upwards, her grip tightens.

"I'm going to take off those cuffs, and you're going to put your hands behind your back, like a good girl."

She doesn't need to threaten. I know what she can do, and if she decides to kill me, then that's what she decides.

"You're going to be a good girl," she says.

She takes the key from the dresser and, holding the knife with her other hand, reaches down to the cuff on my left wrist. The key clicks against the metal and her eyes swivel towards me. "Like this?" she asks, and twists the key in the air.

"Yes."

While she fiddles with the lock I try to breathe, to calm myself, and to evoke the cold calm.

I need to pull myself out of this mire, even if only temporarily. I should live for the twins, even if it's only to survive this girl's intrusion before taking my own life afterwards.

Stuart.

Declan.

Gone.

The left-side handcuffs click open, and my numb arm falls to the bed.

"You," she says, holding out the key.

"I can't move my arm. It's dead."

The girl's face flickers. "Dead." She goes to the other side of the bed and works the key into the other lock. After a second, briefer struggle, my hand falls from the bedpost, immobile.

She looks at me, and one side of her red-smeared mouth becomes an almost-smile. "Bend over the bed and give me your hands."

I shuffle my stiff legs to the side and hang them over

the mattress, my knees inches from hers. Circulation slowly returns to my arms.

"This is what daddies make good girls do," she says.

I turn around, wary, and lay my face and breasts against bedcovers soaked in my husbands' blood.

The twins watch us sullenly from the bathroom.

"It's okay, Phil, Lilith!" I call out, weakly. "We're just playing!"

I place my wrists together at the base of my spine, imagining how the knife would feel penetrating me.

My right buttock stings from a sharp but fleeting impact.

"You like that," the girl says. Her hand returns to my spanked ass, squeezing the flesh. "You like that, don't you?"

Metal clamps my wrists behind me. I feel what must be the edge of the blade scratch the length of my spine, down towards the upper cleft of my buttocks.

"If I was a daddy, I'd fuck you good," she says.

It's impossible to tell if she is making a point or enjoying her control over me. I await the sharp metal, but instead she takes hold of my hair and wrenches me upwards. I press a foot flat against the floor, rising to a half-kneel. I can tell that she will keep dragging even if I remain on my knees.

My dead son Declan seems to watch as I stand, his eyes dull white marbles. There lies the first child into whom I had planted my hopes, my loves, my plans and my morals, motionless beside the corpse of my husband, my protector, whose genes he shares.

Shared.

The girl steps in front of me, obscuring my view of the

bodies. "Do you have clothes?"

"I…" I begin, having never been asked such a question. "In the wardrobe."

The girl frowns.

"Over there," I say, nodding towards the corner by the door.

Leaving me upright, naked and handcuffed, the girl raises a leg over my mutilated husband. When she pulls open both wardrobe doors her eyes fill with wonder, as if she is operating high-tech equipment from another world.

Across the hall, the twins splash each other in unnatural silence.

The girl selects an elegant charcoal grey chemise that will be too large for her, and a pair of white jeans that have too many silver buckles to match the top. She holds the clothes out, inspecting them. Her underbite hangs ajar. With care, but obvious inexperience, she tugs the items from their hangers before dropping the hangers to the carpet. As she turns the fabrics over in her hands, she stains them with my family's blood.

I picture her corpse, clad in my clothes.

"Do you like them?" I ask.

She looks up, face unreadable, and nods.

"You can put them on," I say. Trying to stay friendly. Trying not to look at my family, both the living and the dead.

Her eyebrows dip in almost Neanderthal confusion. She turns the clothes around in her hands.

"Do you need help … putting them on?"

She bundles the items into a fist and steps towards me, one of her bare feet pressing into the palm of my husband's lifeless hand. "I'm going to teach you about daddies, and you can teach me about clothes." She lifts the knife, prods its point against my left breast. "And you're going to be a good girl."

I nod. "Yes."

Jonathan Butcher

17. Girl

The Girl who was on the bed tells me to take off her handcuffs. I step behind her and hold the metal thing against her backbone. It's hard opening the handcuffs using just one hand.

When they're off, she turns around and tells me, "If you put the knife down, you won't cut the clothes when I help you put them on. I'm going to be a Good Girl. I promise."

Daddy once told me that Girls lie a lot, so I say, "No. Just help me put them on."

She frowns and ducks down to the floor, helping me to step into the leg-clothes. She pulls them up around my waist and sticks them together just above my nice smooth cunt. Next she pulls the top-clothes down around my neck. I put my arms into the tubes one at a time, switching the metal thing, which she had called a "knife", between my hands as I go.

Her clothes feel better than warm water against my skin. Better than scratching the Bad away. Even though it feels different against my cunt and my skin, it's like being wrapped in bedcovers while I'm standing up.

"Do you like them?" the Girl who was on the bed asks.

She sounds nice. It makes me think of when I had hugged her and she had kissed my cheek.

Mother.

I nod. "Yes, I like them."

"Do you want to see?"

I look down.

"In a mirror, I mean."

I once read a book where a Daddy fucked a Girl in front of a mirror. They watched each other while he fucked her. The book said that a mirror shows a reflection, like the water sometimes does in my toilet and in my sink. After I had read the book, I had asked My Daddy if he had a mirror for me. He just said, "Don't be silly. Good Girls don't need mirrors to know that they're beautiful. Good Girls believe what their Daddies say."

The Girl from the bed says, "Come this way."

I follow her to the bathroom, where the little Girl and the little Daddy are splashing together. They stop when I reach the doorway.

The Girl from the bed makes a shaky, different smile, and points at the wall. "Here."

I step inside. There is a screen on the wall, and another Girl standing up inside the screen.

The Girl in the screen has the same face as the Girl from the bed.

"You look ... lovely," the Girl from the bed says. The

Girl in the screen opens and closes her mouth, like she's saying the same words. "Look."

I reach out. A hand in the screen reaches for my fingers. I've seen pictures like this in my sink and toilet, but those ones wobble and shake and swirl. I snatch my hand back, but then reach out again and touch the screen. It feels like my TV screen did, before I broke it on My Daddy's head. When I'm touching the mirror, the reflection-hand touches my fingers. I know it's just a picture, like when I see movements in the sink and in the toilet, but it makes me want to scream.

The Girl from the bed moves sideways, away from me. I swallow because I feel different, but then I stand next to her.

A smaller Girl appears in the mirror.

The new, smaller Girl is not pretty like the Girls in the films. She has red stuff across her mouth and her jaw sticks out. Her eyes are really close together. Her hair is long but flat.

The Girls in the films always look really happy or really shaky and different when they're being fucked, but the Girl in the mirror just looks sleepy. Her ugly face crinkles like a screwed-up blanket, and her eyes go small and wet. I want to break the mirror but I just stand there. When I start to cry, the ugly Girl in the mirror cries, too.

I feel the Girl from the bed's hand on my shoulder. I turn her way because I don't want to look at the other Girl in the mirror. I don't want to look at *me*.

What I want is for the Girl from the bed to kiss and hug me, and to tell me, "Sssshhh, everything will be okay."

"I'm Serenity," the Girl from the bed says. "And these two are Phillip and Lilith." She points at the little ones in the thing filled with water.

"Serenity," I say.

I look down at the little Daddy and the little Girl in the water. Serenity rubs my back. I want her to kiss me again, but I also want to cry and lie down in a ball and kill all the Daddies, or maybe just go back to My Room and fall asleep and never wake up.

"You don't have to hurt anyone else," Serenity says, as she touches my shoulder.

The little Girl, Lilith, starts to cry, too. I turn around. Her little body shivers.

The little Daddy, Phillip, reaches up towards my knife.

"No, sweetie," Serenity says, and pushes Phillip's hand away.

"I don't know what to do," I say.

"There are people who can help. Not everyone wants to hurt you. Not all men are Bad."

"All the daddies ... *the men* ... want to fuck me. They want to fuck you, too."

She stops rubbing me. "Stuart and Declan were Good men." Her face looks like it's going to break. "Phillip, here, is almost two years old," she says, pointing to the little Daddy in the water. "If Lilith falls over, Phillip strokes her hair and kisses her better. He is *innocent* – do you know what that means? It means that he's ... that the world hasn't corrupted him. Broken him. All he wants to do is play with his sister, and laugh when she cries, and cry when she laughs." She coughs. It sounds like crying. "If I keep teaching Phillip how to behave, how to be a Good man, then Phillip will grow up and *be* a Good man."

I don't understand every word, but I understand most of them. I understand enough to know that she's wrong, so I turn to her, run my fingers up her arm, and then lock them around her throat.

Serenity's eyes go really, really big when I lift the knife up to her tits.

I say, "I'm sorry, Serenity. But you don't know Daddies like I do."

Jonathan Butcher

18. Serenity

When the girl grabs my throat, I realise the courage that it would take to resist her. I don't want my children to watch me die, so I stand stock still and hope that she doesn't push the knife any harder against my breast.

"You don't believe me about daddies," the girl says, and yanks me through the doorway by the neck. "But you will."

I let her drag me into the hall, noticing a strange animation touch her face for the first time. Despite the fact that she's still holding the blade, her urgency reminds me of a child pulling a classmate towards somewhere new and exciting.

At the top of the stairs, I bat her hand away and stop following her. "Don't make me leave the twins."

When she turns, the playful child in her has vanished.

Her brow slants downwards, her eyes narrow and she bares her teeth. I almost dive sideways and slam the bathroom door, just to put a sheet of wood between myself and this child-girl, who is clad in my mismatched clothes and smeared with my family's blood.

"*You're a bad girl,*" she hisses, but when she pushes the knife point against the swell of my left breast again, I stand firm.

"Please," I pant, matching her stare but striving to remain passive, unthreatening. "This can't just go on and on. It has to stop somewhere."

Her face does not alter and the knife does not move.

I ask, "If I go with you, are you going to…make me go to sleep?"

"If you're bad."

"Then where do you want to take me?"

"To my daddy's big place. Down to my room."

"For what? To teach me about men? About 'daddies'?"

She nods. "They tell us that we like it, don't they?"

She flips the blade around and lifts it higher so that it is aimed, handle-first, towards my face.

"They say, 'You like that, don't you?' And then they hurt you."

Before I realise what she is going to do, she rams the handle into my cheek. A silver streak of pain lances through my skull. It's a restrained blow, though, like a pulled movie-punch, and in some vague manner it reminds me of Stuart spanking me.

"They say, 'Good girl'."

The handle falls again, slamming into my chin. It smarts, but does no real damage.

From the bath, Phillip and Lilith wail in unison.

"They say, 'Show me that tight asshole' and, 'Show me your nice smooth cunt'. Then they burn you, or break you."

The girl hits me with the handle twice more, once on either cheek. I suspect that if I were to flinch or fight back, she would turn the blade on me.

"And then they fuck you and make you say that you like it, even when you don't. Or, worse, *they make you like it*."

The knife handle collides with the centre of my forehead. The sting tells me that this is a different kind of blow, and has broken the skin. I brace myself for more.

"You're a good girl, Serenity," she says. "But girls should only like other girls, and you still don't think that your daddy was like mine."

My head reels from the pain of my weirdly consensual beating. When I picture Stuart bleeding and lying flat against the girl's back, I let out a sob.

"I'll show you, though, Serenity," the girl says. "I'll show you what daddies do."

She pulls the knife back again, and I say, "Please."

She holds it there, ready to strike.

"Please," I repeat. "Tell me that if I follow you, you won't make me go to sleep."

Something flickers across her face.

"Promise me," I urge. "Promise me that afterwards, if I'm good, I can come back here and take care of my babies."

"Promise?"

Absurdly, I raise my fist with the pinkie extended, as if making a deal with a child. "Yes, promise. It means that you mean it and you can't lie."

She lifts her empty hand, mirroring my gesture, and I wrap my pinkie around hers. Something subtle in her face tells me that she understands.

"Okay," she says.

For a long moment, her eyes are no longer the empty wells I've become used to. I wonder if she's going to embrace me, but she doesn't. Her eyes shimmer, gazing out from a face defined by scabbed blood. For a second she is almost beautiful.

"Promise," she says, and releases my finger.

19. Girl

I didn't want to hit Serenity so much, but she needed it. Now her cheeks are rosy and cute, and there's a thin line of red stuff running down her nose.

"Can I put on some clothes first?" she asks.

"Good Girls don't wear clothes." I take hold of her neck with one hand and say, "Open your mouth."

When she does, I stuff her lacy cunt-clothes between her lips. I don't think she is going to scream or try to run away, but I want to make sure.

My Daddy and some of the other Daddies like tying me up, and sometimes I practise knots on my bedclothes. I tie some of Serenity's see-through leg-clothes around her face. Now she can't spit out the cunt-clothes.

"Follow me," I tell her, and lead her down the stairs.

Walking downwards is harder than going up. I feel like I'm going to trip and fall and break my head.

Serenity comes slowly down behind me. I keep looking back at her and she keeps looking back up the stairs, back towards the room with the little Daddy Phillip and the little Girl Lilith. We get to the bottom and I feel confused for a second, but then I turn and walk into the big room. There are chairs that look like beds, plus tall wooden things and a big TV. The room's screen doors are still open, their long white screen-clothes flapping in the moving air.

We step through the screen doors and onto the square of tickly green stuff. I don't want to look up at the blue ceiling, with its white patches and the really bright light. I take Serenity's wrist, even though she is already following me, but then I slip my fingers lower and hold onto her hand.

The little thing with four legs and yellow eyes, which I think is a dog, looks out from one of the big green things beside the wall.

"Murph," Serenity says.

Murph the dog disappears.

Serenity makes a whiny noise, like the ones that I sometimes make when I've had enough biting or hitting. I lead her across the tickly green stuff and push open a big wooden wall-door with my knife hand. I think that this will take us round to My Daddy's big place.

I squeeze Serenity's hand and she squeezes mine back, but when I look at her face she's got narrow eyes, like a Bad Girl. I look around the corner of the wooden wall-door into the long room that smells like piss, the one where I'd found the little Daddy playing with his yellow car, which is lying on the floor upside down. I can see real cars at both ends and patches of the little Daddy's red stuff on the ground. There are also more buzzing bugs, and two little black things that jump up towards the blue ceiling when they see me, twitching their arms as they go.

A big Girl's voice calls from somewhere close, "Martiiiiiiin! Martiiiiiiiiin!"

My belly goes, SQUISH.

I don't want Serenity to see the little Daddy covered in red stuff, so when I push open the wall-door that I hope will take us to My Daddy's big place, I let go of her hand and hold mine over her eyes, leading her with my knife hand pressed against her lower back.

Some bugs, black and twitchy, have landed on the little Daddy's face. He must have opened his eyes while I was away. It's like he's staring at me, and even though he's little and I'm wearing Serenity's clothes, I feel like he wants to fuck me.

I pull Serenity towards the door made of screens at the side of My Daddy's big place. I feel like I'm going to puke again, but I'm better once we get the screen door open. I take my hand off Serenity's eyes and we step into the room filled with shiny metal things.

Serenity looks around, blinking. I pull the see-through leg-clothes up off her mouth and reach two fingers between her lips. She coughs when I take out her cunt-clothes, and makes her lips go, PUH, PUH, PUH.

"You live here?" she asks.

I shake my head.

"Then why are we…"

I go to the door that opens to the really, really small room, open it and point inside.

"In the cupboard?" Serenity asks. She wipes some red stuff off her nose.

89

In the really small room there are glass things that smell like food, shiny papery things, long pieces of wood, and small metal things that are different to my knife. I step into the dark and push the back wall. It opens a bit.

Serenity breathes in behind me.

I start to walk inside, but then I think that I should point the knife at Serenity or she might not follow me.

"I … don't want to…" Serenity says. Her face is puffy and her lips are shaking.

"I want you to see," I tell her, but now *I'm* feeling shaky and different, too. "Then you can tell me if Daddies are Bad or not."

In the Other Film, the two Girls never, ever hurt each other. They just kiss and they hug and make red stuff come out of all the Daddies. I look at Serenity and I wonder, do I look like she looks when Daddies fuck me? When they hit me, does *my* face go puffy? And do I look at their cocks the way that Serenity looks at my knife?

Serenity stands there shaking her head, with her eyes wet and shiny. "I'm worried about Phillip. And Lilith." She lets out a horrid, "BLUH!" sound, and a white bubble pops at one side of her mouth.

I say, "After you come down here and see My Room, you can go back to them. Promise."

She looks me in the eyes. I can smell her sweet fruity skin as she steps past me into the really small room, pushes the moving wall all the way open, and steps inside.

20. Serenity

My face still throbs from the beating that the girl had given me.

She had covered my eyes as she had led me into what I assume was her back garden, and when she took her hands away I was standing in a homely, old-fashioned kitchen, with plain white cupboards, metal cooking utensils hanging from the walls and a square wooden clock. It had smelled like freshly baked pastry.

Mr Crisp's kitchen.

Or, *our kindly old next-door neighbour*, as I had called him just an hour or so ago.

The kitchen's walk-in cupboard is filled with jars of herbs, brooms, sweeps, DIY tools, and things encased in plastic wrapping, but beyond these there is a fake wall. When I push it all the way open, it reveals a set of downward steps, bordered by walls padded with a foam-like substance no doubt to make them soundproof. A strip-light is mounted above the staircase, illuminating walls dimpled with humps and hillocks.

As I descend, I'm half-convinced that I am never going to see daylight again. The stairs through the fake wall are carpeted, and as I progress I hold my hands against the bannister that leads along the padded left wall. At the bottom there is a thick door, the kind that I imagine could secure a bank vault. It stands ajar. When I push, it opens with a sound like whirring cogs.

Inside there is a room of about 20 by 30 feet. In contrast to the care with which someone had ensured that the outer staircase remains protected and hidden from the house above, this room smells dank and uncared for. The ceiling is a mesh of bare pipes, while the red-brick walls are a looped riot of crayon scrawls. There is no carpet; only kitchen-style floor tiles.

I'm about to step inside when a disturbing new thought hits me: the girl sealing me inside. I gesture for her to lead the way, and she does so without hesitation.

I test the heavy door to ensure that it is unlikely to swing back of its own volition, and then step into the room.

The first thing I notice is the prostrate body lying beside a shattered TV. Its half-demolished face is pin-cushioned with splinters of glass. Its head is surrounded by a bloody moat. The zipper of its light brown chinos is open, a morsel of red meat poking out. Scraps of what could be muscle or flesh sprinkle the hard, blood-dotted floor to the body's side. One of its hands stretches towards me, its smallest finger curled back on itself, like the opposite to a pinkie promise.

Kindly Mr Crisp.

A long bookshelf on the wall behind the bed reveals titles such as "Branded For Daddy", "Cry For Me", and "A Whore and a Virgin". Piled like book-ends at either end of the row are two stacks of pornographic magazines. The cover at the top of the left-hand pile shows a close-up of the face of a crying teenage girl wearing pigtails. A black-gloved hand clutches her throat. A white gobbet hangs from one of her cheeks. On the right-hand pile, the top cover shows a spread vulva, each labia pierced three times by hooks on thin chains. They tug the lips apart in a way that makes me wince, revealing the tender, glistening pink inside.

I follow the crayon scribbles along the wall to a desk and a chair, where there is a notepad and a colour-coordinated line of crayons in an oblong pencil tin.

I open the notepad and read the first page's four-word title, handwritten in blue crayon in surprisingly neat script: *What Good Girls Do.*

I feel the girl watching me as I flick through the pages. An artist – presumably the girl – has used pink, red and brown crayons to depict the same naked girl on each page. She has long dark hair, detailed breasts and genitalia, but she does not have a face; only a pink, featureless scribble. Black silhouettes penetrate the crayon-girl's scrawled body with their shadowy fingers and penises, or choke her, or push her against the floor. The further into the notepad that I flick, the more frequently the red crayon replaces the pink of the crayon-girl's body.

I let the book close and glance at the girl, whose usually-blank face has softened. Her eyes seem more curious than I've seen them before, perhaps measuring me up.

Next along, at the foot of the desk, there is a pink yoga mat.

The girl says, "My daddy showed me a film where a girl is doing what my daddy called exercises, and then a daddy comes along and slaps her face and fucks her tight ass and makes her taste the shit off his cock. I asked My Daddy if I could have a mat to do exercises on, and my daddy said okay."

There are two waist-high DVD cabinets to my left. I can barely stomach reading them, but I'm left in no doubt as to the discs' content. The side of one states "Broken Girls #5", while another simply reads, "Raped". For some reason, the hand-scrawled title of "Tina" on one black, picture-less case makes me want to vomit.

I notice another DVD on the floor beside the bed. While its cover of an abused, naked woman is aesthetically similar to the filth lining the walls, this is a movie that I'm actually familiar with. It's a low-budget, ultra-feminist revenge film, in which two abused women launch an all-out assault against the male gender. "Raw, emotional, and cathartic", declares a critic's quote on the cover. I'd thought that it was exploitative trash.

The girl says, "My Daddy comes down here and shows me the films and fucks my nice smooth cunt and brings me food and reads the stories with me."

"Those?" I ask, pointing at the books beside her bed.

She nods.

"Did...your daddy...*ever* let you out?"

"This is *my room*," she says, emphasizing the two words.

She stares at me, her face finally revealing something

raw, perhaps truthful. "Good girls let their daddy's keep them safe. 'Don't be silly', my daddy always said. 'Be a good girl'. And then he would fuck me and choke me and let my other daddies fuck me and hit me and feed me their hard cocks and..." She bites her lip. "That's what daddies do."

Again I experience that dreadful Orwellian "doublethink". For one part, I want this girl to suffer for what she did to my son and my husband, and how *dare* she act upset and hurt when she's a fucking *murderer*? But another side of my brain wants to reach out to her. If what she tells me is true – and all I have seen suggests that it is – then perhaps she is simply a product of all she knows, and has never been shown an alternative.

"Honey," I say, hating the word as it leaves my mouth. "Not *all* men are like your daddies."

I think of Stuart's firm touch. How safe I'd always felt with him. His hands closing around my throat.

I survey the room again, at the porn and the notepad and the blood-soaked corpse. My stomach contents seem to curdle when I notice a security camera positioned near the door, between the wall and ceiling. It points at the bed, and a red light above the lens blinks languidly, watching us.

"Daddy's eye," the girl says.

I shiver, remembering my last encounter with Mr Crisp. We had moved to this neighbourhood four years ago, after Stuart had received a pay rise. Our neighbour had always been proud of his front garden. One morning last week, Mr Crisp had been clipping the spherical hedge at the end of his driveway, stood beside his navy blue classic Jaguar. He had nodded at me and tipped an invisible hat as I had passed, a smile stretched across his broad face, the sunlight catching in his grey hair.

I ask the girl, "Do you remember *anything*, apart than this room?"

"I think there was another a girl here, once."

"A girl like you?"

"A bigger girl. I asked my daddy, but he just said, 'Don't be silly'."

She's no longer holding the blade in a threatening manner. I could probably take four steps backwards and slam the door, get out of this hellhole and back to my babies, but what if she gets to me first?

"I meant what I said," I tell her. "I can find people who can help you. Girls. Women. People who won't, as you say, want to...fuck you."

She looks at me with those lightless eyes; sunken, distrusting pebbles. "Do you believe me? About the daddies?"

I give no reply but I picture Stuart's face as he'd struggled to secure her earlier: triumph, with an unmistakable hint of lust. Even Declan's eyes, just minutes before he'd died, had flickered similarly as they roved across this girl's bloody, filth-encrusted body.

"Are there *really* girls who can make me better?" the girl asks, stepping towards me. "Girls who will hug me, and not want to fuck me?"

"Yes."

She frowns, rubs a flake of dried blood from her chin with the sleeve of her knife arm. She seems to notice the blade and hesitates.

Before she decides what to do next, a noise comes from outside the door. We freeze, and the low murmur rises into a grumbled chorus.

Panic ignites inside me.

The voices continue, identifying themselves as male.

The girl answers my question before I ask it. "My other daddies."

Jonathan Butcher

21. Girl

My other daddies are coming.

I know them all, and I know what they like to do. I feel really, REALLY shaky and different, but not just for me this time – for Serenity.

Before I had left My Room, I had always let them do whatever they'd wanted, because that's what Good Girls do. Now, though, I don't ever want their cocks inside my nice smooth cunt or my tight ass again. Now, I want to hit them with my knife. I want to bite through their cocks. I want them all to sleep and never wake up.

Upstairs, I hear my Skinny Daddy yell, "Jeff!"

Serenity's eyes bulge.

The second voice, crackly and deep, is my Cigarette Daddy. "He won't hear you if he's already down there with her."

"Fuck's sake, *I* was supposed to be first today," Skinny

Daddy says.

A third voice sounds thick but smooth, and makes me think of lube. He's the worst one: my Red Daddy. "He should have met us up here. He'd never leave it open like this."

I turn to Serenity and lift my finger to my lips, like one of the Daddies does in the film where the Girl keeps saying, "No no no," whenever she gets hit. I hold on to the knife with one hand and push Serenity towards the bathroom door with the other. Her eyes get even bigger, as if they want to eat up her face, but she steps away from me and into my bathroom, shaking her head.

"The door is open!" Cigarette Daddy shouts. "*Jeff?*"

I think that the Daddies are going to come down here and see My Daddy, all covered in red stuff. Then, I think that they are going to make the red stuff come out of my cunt, and then out of Serenity's cunt, and then they are going to make us both go to sleep.

While my other Daddies' feet get louder on the stairs, I close the bathroom door on Serenity really, really quietly. Then I turn around and face the door to My Room.

The first Daddy that comes through the door is Cigarette Daddy, the fat one who likes to put out cigarettes on my tongue. Cigarette Daddy sees me, and sees My Daddy all covered in red stuff, and says, "Oh shit oh shit oh shit."

I rush at him. He falls against the door with a CRAK. I grab his shoulder and stick the knife into his fat stomach.

He says, "Uck."

I pull my knife out and then push it in again even quicker, just like I did with the little Daddy who had the yellow car. Red stuff pours out over my hand really, really fast. I pull the knife out and push it in again, counting 1, 2, 3, 4, but when I reach 4, Cigarette Daddy's knees bend. They go KUNCH. His head flops forwards and he goes limp. I rip the knife out and the door bangs open again and he sort of slides down it, his eyes blinking and his torn belly pissing out red stuff over his leg-clothes and the floor.

"Christ, stay back!" Red Daddy says from the stairs. I think about jumping out the door and trying to put the knife into the next Daddy, too, but I don't.

"Go go go!" Red Daddy says.

I hear their footsteps going back up the stairs, and poke my head around the door.

Red Daddy is walking backwards up the stairs, touching the bumpy walls on both sides. "You little whore," he says when he sees me. His eyes are squished almost closed behind his thick black glasses, like little Girls' cunts.

"What's she done?" Skinny Daddy asks. He is all shadowy because he is already in the really small room at the top of the stairs.

Skinny Daddy likes to stop me breathing with his cock and his hands. He always smells like damp bedclothes. Once, he tried to put his whole foot into my mouth and made me puke, and afterwards, he said, "Good Girl."

Red Daddy says, "Little bitch has *done* Sparky. Now shut up and listen…"

They disappear into the darkness of the little room at the top of the stairs.

Cigarette Daddy sits leaning against the door to My Room. He coughs. A dark red bubble pops between his lips. He says "UCK" again, breathes out, and closes his eyes.

101

I hold onto my knife really tightly, like a Daddy holding onto his big hard cock. I listen for the other two Daddies, but there's nothing. Serenity hasn't opened the bathroom door, which is Good. Maybe if I try really hard I can help Serenity get back to her big place, before my other Daddies make me go to sleep.

I promised her.

I go over to My Daddy and reach into his leg clothes. Some glass falls off, TINK TINK TINK. I feel around against his leg and my fingers touch something small and cold.

I hear my other Daddies' voices again. They're coming. They want to fuck me and make me go to sleep for being a Bad Girl.

I feel really shaky and different, but I don't think I will mind if they call me a Bad Girl now.

I don't want to be a Good Girl, anymore.

22. Serenity

The best weapon that I can find in the bathroom is the toilet cistern lid, just as Declan had used on the girl before she had taken his life. I hold the lid with a hand on either of its sides and imagine swinging it into the back of the girl's neck.

I have always been very aware of my body states, so I know precisely what is happening as I descend deeper into shock. I feel nauseated and faint, and my heart feels like the fluttering wing of a panicked insect, but I won't pass out; I'm too fucking alert and too fucking conscious of my son and daughter, sat alone in a cold bath just a minute's walk away.

In this tiny bathroom there is a shower cubicle and a toilet, both of which are clean and mildew-free, despite the ceiling being a gnarl of bare copper pipes, just like the bedroom. The walls are papered with peeling images of animated Asian pornography: bug-eyed schoolgirls being violated by leering, drooling, white-haired men.

Being careful to make as little sound as possible, I lean the cistern lid against the wall to the right of the door, and then take a look through the keyhole. I can only see a narrow slice of the room beyond, but can define the girl's grey-dressed shoulder and one side of her face, just a few feet away. She appears to be crouching above Mr Crisp's corpse, which lies out of my view. I think she's rifling through its pockets. Having apparently found whatever she had wanted, she rises and vanishes again so that I can only see the body of the man that she had stabbed lying slumped against the crayon-marked far wall. His chin rests on his chest, as if he's inspecting his belly's drooling puncture wounds.

There is a soft but sharp clatter of metal against something solid, followed by a brief jangle. The girl reappears and sits down cross-legged and straight-backed on the floor in the centre of the room, facing the doorway.

I hear my shallow breaths and struggle to regulate them. If I stay here, I will be found. If I leave, though, I will be killed, either by the girl or by the men who were here moments ago and are presumably still upstairs, plotting their next move. I want to scream out to the girl through the keyhole, to order her to stand up and fight these men on my behalf.

Someone else enters the bedroom. I can't see them, but I hear, "What have you done, you wretched little cunt?"

"Why … why doesn't she go for us, too?" a second, higher voice asks.

"Coz that's not what good girls do, is it? Have you

remembered your place now, girl?"

"Fuck, Sparky."

"Leave him."

"But…"

"Even if he isn't dead, we aren't going to the hospital."

The girl – who is still the only person I can see through the keyhole – remains still. She looks ridiculous in my baggy clothes, but somehow undefeated. I don't think that she is even looking at them.

"What did you do?" the deeper-voiced one asks.

The weaker-sounding one spits, "*We're talking to you, cunt!*"

A boot thrusts into view and connects with the girl's cheek. Her head snaps sideways, propelling her into the bedframe before she sprawls flat across the floor. I cover my mouth.

"*Bad girl!*" her attacker yells, his voice shrill as his legs and waist step into view. A long finger stabs the air above the crumpled girl. "*Very … bad … GIRL!*"

"It's over, Darryl."

"Where'd you get those fuckin' clothes?" her attacker demands. He crouches and I see a long, angular face.

"Darryl, did you hear what I said?" the other one asks. "We have to clear up."

Darryl grunts, his shoulders sagging. "Really?"

"There was always going to come a day. She's getting older now, anyway. All that hair."

Skinny guy Darryl kneels beside her. He throws a sharp downwards jab and there's a thud. "You hear that? No longer any use. Good girls are best before they bleed, aren't they? And you're *way* past that."

"You stay here and do what's got to be done," the man

who I still haven't seen tells Darryl. "I'll take care of things upstairs and then head out for fuel. Then we'll need to take them upstairs."

"Shit," Darryl mutters. "We'll have to dump the car."

I hear the other man laugh. He sounds like a hearty drinker in an ale house. "It's like a sale, Darryl: everything must go! *Everything must go.*"

Darryl sighs. "Cuffs."

A hand appears from the right, passing Darryl a pair of handcuffs. The sight of them makes me think of Stuart, but now is not the time for sorrow, or for nostalgia. Now is the time for last-minute prayers or urgent plans of action, but I haven't the strength for either.

I'm frozen, unconvinced that I'll ever be able to move again. So, helpless, I watch.

23. Girl

If I'm going to go to sleep and not wake up, Serenity should see what my other Daddies do. So when Red Daddy leaves My Room and Skinny Daddy handcuffs my wrists in front of me and turns me over so that I am on my knees and hands, I let him do it, just like normal.

"One more ride," Skinny Daddy says.

I hear him fiddle with his leg-clothes and then something hits my ass with a WHAP.

"You're going to be my Good Girl, one last time, aren't you?"

He pulls the leg-clothes down around my thighs.

"Good Girls don't wear clothes, remember?" he says from behind me.

He hits me again: WHAP.

"You like that, don't you?"

I say nothing. Nothing at all.

"Did your daddy buy you those clothes? He was always too soft on you. Is that what made you flip out?"

Something presses against my nice tight cunt, soft but getting harder.

"Maybe you were never a Good Girl at all," Skinny Daddy says. "Maybe you think you're smart. Maybe you were thinking about getting that old sod for a long, long time."

The thing touching my cunt has grown. It pushes a bit, opening me.

"Want to look at what you did while I fuck you? Want to suck that broken glass off your daddy's face while I cum?"

I feel his fingers wrap around my neck, pulling me backwards. It hurts my wrists, because of the cuffs pressing them together.

Skinny Daddy always likes to choke me, but what Skinny Daddy *doesn't* usually do is wrap his stiff waist-clothes around my throat, and squeeze.

My eyes feel like they are going to break and I feel like I'm going to puke. I can't breathe so I can't puke either, even though I make a puking sound as he pulls.

"Wanted to do this for a while now, girl," Skinny Daddy says.

I hardly hear him because he's shoved his big hard cock into my nice tight cunt and I can't breathe, I can only make little squishy noises as if I'm cocksucking, but I'm not, and I never will again.

I hope Serenity is watching from the bathroom, through the keyhole. I hope she sees this.

Skinny Daddy has one hand on my shoulder, and the other one must be pulling the waist-clothes that he's wrapped around my neck. He drags me upwards and the room goes cloudy and dark.

My cuffed hands are wobbling and I don't feel shaky and different anymore. I just want to go to sleep and not wake up, but if I move my body backwards, maybe the thing around my neck will loosen a bit. Skinny Daddy's cock is inside me, though, so there's nowhere for me to go.

I let my arms bend and fall forwards onto my elbows. The waist-clothes tighten, so I can't even make cocksucking noises anymore. My Room is getting so dark that I can't even see the clouds, I can only see little black patches, and I know I'm falling asleep.

"Already?" Skinny Daddy says, from the darkness. "Fuck, *come on.* You can last longer than that."

The waist-clothes loosen a little so I suck in lots of air, and instead of falling asleep I stretch my arms out and reach my hands forwards, really far. It must look like I'm being a Good Girl and stretching out for him, but I'm not. I'm being a very, very Bad Girl, because even though the room has gone black and I can't see anything, I've got a hold on the knife, which I'd hidden under the bed.

"Oh, fuck yeah," Skinny Daddy says, and the waist-clothes tighten around my neck again.

Something in my throat goes TIKK, but he doesn't pull me up. He doesn't say anything about the knife, either, so maybe he has closed his eyes. I drop down onto my face and tits and reach my cuffed arms backwards under my belly, as if I'm going to rub his balls and help him cum. Instead of that though, I point the knife towards my shaved cunt and, with My Room all black and my chest feeling tighter than the tightest tight, I shove the blade upwards, really hard.

There's a soft KUNCH and a really big pain, but that's okay. I'm Good at taking pain. I push the knife up even higher, up through the skin to the inside of my nice smooth cunt.

Skinny Daddy does a weird gurgle. He stops fucking me and moans. The waist-clothes go loose around my neck and suddenly something breaks my nice round ass, not like a spank, but like a fist.

"What … the … *fuck?*" Skinny Daddy squeaks.

Something keeps breaking my ass. I think he's trying to really hurt me. I give the knife one more push, and it feels like it did when Red Daddy had made the red stuff come out of my cunt that time, but more painful. *Better.*

"*What did you do?*" Skinny Daddy whispers.

I can see a little bit again, so I ram my ass backwards, just like I had when Serenity's Daddy Stuart had been trying to fuck me in the other big place. There's a tearing sound. Skinny Daddy blows out a really big breath. He breaks my ass again, but then I feel him holding my waist to try and keep me still. This time, though, I pull away, *hard.* The pain in my cunt grows really REALLY REALLY big, and it's bigger and better than cigarette burns, better than hitting My Daddy with the TV, and even better than when Serenity had kissed and hugged me and made me feel warm.

Skinny Daddy lets go of me. He's making high squeaky sounds. I use the bed covers to pull myself forwards, up onto my knees. When I turn around, I can feel his big cock getting soft inside my nice smooth cunt, even though he's holding the place between his legs where it used to be and there's red stuff splashing all over his hands and legs.

The room is still cloudy. I want to sleep because the pain just keeps getting worse and better and worse and better, but I don't sleep, not yet.

Instead, I smile, because I've scratched my Skinny Daddy's Bad away.

Jonathan Butcher

24. Serenity

I witness the scene with my hands clamped over my mouth, too numb to do anything except stare through the keyhole.

Throughout the girl's ordeal, I could see little more than her tail and the thrusting of Darryl's hips. The ugliest thing about the rape was how closely it resembled the everyday submissive sex that I have consented to hundreds of times before: no screams, no struggle, and a leather belt constricting a throat. But this time it's being perpetrated upon a vulnerable, childlike, murderous young woman, in the bedroom-cell that I assume she has spent her life being abused in – until today.

I saw the upward jerk of her hands. I had only realised that something had altered between them when the man had begun to punch her backside. She had dragged her tailbone away from him, revealing a blink of metal and a sudden surge of blood. Before his hands had time to cup the flow, I had glimpsed the red-spewing stump that remained between his legs.

This sight alongside the man's strange mewls awakens me from my stupor.

I had only heard three voices coming from outside, so does that mean that there is only one more threat in the house? Or is the girl a danger to me as well?

Regardless, I heave the toilet lid up from the ground, brace myself at the door, and say a silent goodbye to my twin babies still sat in the bath in my home, just a minute away.

You're both *survivors. If you have to, you'll survive without me.*

Holding the lid with one shaky arm to my chest, I thrust the door open.

The girl is leaning over the bed, perhaps bent double with agony. The man is still kneeling, jeans down, grimacing. Blood gushes between the gaps in his fingers at his crotch. His mouth drops open as he sees me – *catching flies*, Stuart might have said – and he frowns, as if performing mental arithmetic.

He has no time to lift his arms before I swing the toilet lid into the centre of his face. His features seem to implode: lips curling into themselves, nose shattering, eyes squeezing shut, cheekbones breaking with a brittle snap. At first he stays kneeling and his arms raise reflexively a second too late, trying to block a blow that has already caved in part of his head. I swing the edge of the toilet lid into his throat. It propels him back towards the wall, his face and the ruins of his genitals slopping waterfalls of blood over the concrete floor. He slides down and lies motionless on his side, perpendicular to his dead companion by the door.

I turn to the girl. She still hasn't changed her crumpled position over the bed. I want to wrap an arm around her, but instead I circle her until I'm standing at her desk. One of her cheeks rests against the bed sheets. Her face is furrowed, her skin a vivid white.

My mouth is so dry that I can barely shape the words: "What did you do?"

She lifts a trembling, scarlet hand in explanation, and then pushes her front up from the bed with a wretched groan.

The handle of her knife juts from her pubic mound, like a lever waiting to be pulled. Her fingers twitch, paused a few inches from the protrusion. It spatters rhythmic red dots over the floor between her knees.

"Don't touch it," I tell her.

If she doesn't reach a hospital soon, I'm convinced that she will die. If I had ever envisioned a revenge for all she has done to my family, it would *never* have been this obscenity.

"Stay still. Look at me."

Kneeling, she looks. Her vacant expression has vanished and her eyes shimmer with sorrow, and in the midst of her agony she is almost beautiful again.

"I'm going to take off your top," I tell her.

If there is a live feed to the camera on the wall, I'm as good as dead.

I believe that to treat stab wounds you're supposed to leave the impaling object alone if possible, to avoid further bleeding. But when the exit wound is internal and in a place such as this, how could I even stem the flow without removing the blade?

"You need to stay as you are, kneeling."

She obeys and two words seep into my head, like a vile prophecy: *Good girl.*

I think that what I'm about to do will be for the best, and not only for her.

Her survival may depend on me slowing the blood until a medical professional tends to her.

My survival may depend on me getting my hands on that knife.

25. Girl

"Lean against the bed," Serenity tells me.

The clouds have gone, but I still can't see her clearly. Serenity doesn't even look like Serenity, anymore. She looks like a shadow.

The pain in my nice smooth cunt is really big, but I'm not feeling shaky or different anymore. Everything moves slowly. I'm trying to stay kneeling up and doing everything that Serenity the Shadow-Girl tells me to do, but it's hard.

"Lift your arms," Serenity the Shadow-Girl says. "I need the top."

I lift my arms and the Shadow-Girl puts her hands against my sides. Even though I can't focus on her, I can still smell her sweet skin. She lifts the top-clothes. They slide against me and it almost feels Good, in spite of all the pain.

"I think you're going to have to stand up, actually."

Her hands go to my armpits, brushing my tits a little.

She doesn't want to fuck me, though. She's not like that. *Girls* aren't like that.

"This is going to hurt."

She pulls on my arms. As I stand up I hear a scream. My cunt feels like it's been fucked by 15 cocks and 15 of My Daddy's buzzing toys, all at the same time.

"Don't fall. Stay as still as you can."

I stay still, even when the Shadow-Girl crouches in front of me and puts her hand onto the knife handle. The pain gets even bigger. My legs go shaky, but the Shadow-Girl had told me to stay still, so I stay still.

Now the Shadow-Girl's head is at the same height as my cunt.

"I don't think I can do this quickly. I think I'll make it worse if I do."

She starts to pull. The 15 cocks and 15 buzzing toys twist and I scream again, I scream and I scream like I sometimes do when one of my Daddies says, "Scream for me, slut." My legs go really, really shaky and the room goes really, really dark, and everything becomes small and gets even slower. I can't remember if I'm awake or sleeping. If I'm sleeping, I wonder if I'm ever going to wake up.

There's a sharp, wet noise and a bright white pain, and when I look down at the Shadow-Girl she is holding my knife.

"You can sit on the bed, now."

I sit on the bed. Everything in My Room looks really far away, like the blue ceiling had when I'd found the big room next to My Daddy's big place. Way down there between my legs, my bedsheets are going red.

The Shadow-Girl pushes open my legs and slides her thumb and her first finger into my cunt. The 15 cocks and

15 toys shake and break and hurt inside me. When she pulls out her fingers, she's holding something that looks like another little finger, except fatter. She drops it and it lands with a PLIT sound. When she looks up at me, she doesn't look like Serenity or even a Shadow-Girl anymore.

She looks like the bigger Girl who I think used to live in My Room with me, the one who used to hug me and make me feel warm. It almost makes me feel safe, but not the kind of "safe" that My Daddy used to talk about. This is a different kind of safe, one where someone wants to help me but not because they want to fuck me.

I think that this bigger Girl just wants to stop the red stuff, and even though everything hurts more than cigarettes or scratching the Bad away, more than choking and hitting, and even though I think I'm going to go to sleep really, really soon and I might not wake up, I think that this is okay. I think that this is the *real* safe.

The bigger Girl pushes part of the top-clothes up into my cunt. I bite my lip really hard and taste red stuff. The bigger Girl folds the other side of the top-clothes over, and pushes it against the shaved red hole that the knife had made above my cunt.

"Push down on that, *hard.*"

I push and the top-clothes go dark red.

The bigger Girl stands up and goes to the door. Through the pain and the black, I remember something.

"Here," I say, pushing the top-clothes down with one hand but pointing towards the bottom of the bed with the other.

The bigger Girl checks underneath the bed and finds what I'd taken from My Daddy's pocket. She goes to the door and slides the key into the lock.

It goes CLA-*CLUNK*.

She turns back to me, and she really *is* the bigger Girl who I sometimes think that I can remember.

What was the word that Serenity had used earlier?
Mother.

She makes me think of My Mother.

"Don't fall asleep," My Mother says to me, standing at the door. "I'm going to get help, so just keep pushing as hard as you can to stop the blood. Think of something Good. Or count, or something. I'll be back."

She pulls the door open.

"Will you *really* be back?" I ask.

My Mother looks at me from far, far away. "Yes."

I lift my hand and make a fist, and point my little finger. "Promise?"

She looks at me for another second. I think that she's going to come back and wrap her little finger around mine, but then she disappears.

My room is just grey stuff and black clouds now. I count 1, 2, 3, 4, 5, 6 up to 15, and then stop. I try to think of something Good, like My Mother told me to, but I can't.

I get up from the bed and the pain almost makes me fall back down. I keep my hand pressed against my cunt and I walk through the black clouds until I can see My Daddy sleeping on the floor.

I don't know why, but I lie down behind him. The bits of broken screen all over the floor feel like fingernails against my skin, like little scratchy kisses. When I put my arm around him, I try to start counting to 15 again, but I can't remember how. Then my whole room goes black and there's nothing else, nothing at all.

26. Serenity

I pad a careful path up the stairs, gripping the blade and holding it before me. I try to focus on Phillip and Lilith, but all I can imagine are my husband and eldest son lying dead, reduced to leaking sacs of blood, and all I anticipate is being used as the thin man had used the girl downstairs.

I'm just five feet, three inches of holes to be fucked.

When I get back to the twins I'll lock us in the bathroom and hold them tightly, and I'll call the emergency services while I rock and squeeze my children to my chest.

At the top of the steps, I put my ear to the door. Pointless. It's fucking soundproof, like the bedroom I've just escaped.

I pull the sturdy metal handle and to my surprise it opens with a padded huff. There's a waft of herbaceous kitchen smells.

There's still no sound, even as I slip through the narrow crack between door and frame. My bare feet touch the gritty floor of the walk-in cupboard. I take three tentative steps, surrounded by jars and plastic bags lit by the strip light in the hidden passage behind me.

Satisfied that I can hear nothing close by, I ease open the cupboard door. The kitchen is lit by sunshine streaming through the tall windows. It's still just an averagely bright, warm summer's day outside.

I edge forwards and turn to the glass door, the portal to my escape no more than 10 steps away.

I'm thinking of those 10 steps as someone grabs a handful of my hair and wrenches me sideways off my feet. It feels as though I've been scalped, the pain so intense that it is almost blinding. My knees jar with the kitchen tiles and I instinctively swing my arm behind me, flailing the knife until someone grips my wrist.

"Drop it," a thick voice says.

The grasp on my lower arm tightens, fingertips intruding between the tendons. My attacker's other hand yanks my hair. There is a juddered clang as my knife hits the metal counter and then the floor.

"Last man standing, eh?" the deep voice says from behind me. "I saw what you did, you know, interfering little cunt. Camera feed. Always streams to the office, even when it isn't filming a show."

Still clamping my wrist and hair, the man hauls me backwards and away from the kitchen towards unknown parts of the house. I hate myself for whimpering, but when I try to spin myself around the man twists my arm up and behind my back. Pain fires through my shoulder, feeling as though my whole arm is going to snap.

"Did Jeff take a shine to you, want you for himself? Is that how the little whore came to turn the tables on him? Your bad influence?"

I'm dragged on my naked backside through a lounge that smells like dust, old books and sweet biscuits. There is a chintzy brown three-piece suite, paintings of farmland, an old-style box TV and a row of near-identical brass clocks above the fireplace.

"Probably think that we're bad guys, don't you?" he says, pulling me in his wake.

I try to push myself up but my legs just kick and slip against the carpet. My foot hits a small circular table and a figurine of some kind topples with a clunk.

"We may as well be heroes, though." He pulls me through another doorway. "Prickly little *bitches* like you think that we're the minority, but let's be honest: youth is the only beautiful thing we've got in this broken fucking world."

I find my breath: "Stop! Let me stand up at least!"

"You aren't going anywhere," he replies, and slams my head against a wall.

Golden stars spray across my vision, and as we reach a wood-panelled corridor, a dangerous smell hits me: something cloying and flammable.

"If we hadn't started this, someone else would've," he says. "And maybe they'd have gone about it in the wrong way: kidnapping random kids. *Then* you lot would *really* be complaining, wouldn't you?"

We reach an office and the smell of fumes thickens. At my feet, beside a filing cabinet, I see a red jerry can with its cap unscrewed.

"Get up," the man says, coming to a halt.

I'm able to pull myself to my feet, but he still holds my hair and wrist.

"You try anything, and I'll make things a *lot* worse than they need to be. I don't care if I should leave ASAP – I'll make sure that you and I have some fun first."

Once I'm standing, my captor drags my head around by the hair and shoves my face towards two old-style computer screens.

"Nice guy, Jeff was, but a cheap bastard," the man whose face I still haven't seen says. "Splashed out for the cameras, a top-line PC and a big wide bandwidth, but still wouldn't buy anything flatscreen. Wouldn't even buy an electronic lock for the girl's room, the silly sod."

One computer screen shows the girl's hidden basement bedroom. The girl is lying on the floor behind Mr Crisp's corpse, not moving.

The other screen shows a spreadsheet filled with male names.

"See that?" the man asks.

I can't help but turn my head to take in his appearance. He's stocky and short with neatly cropped chocolate-coloured hair, wearing a pale blue shirt and thick-rimmed specs around a pair of almost kind-looking eyes. He seems anxious, a little short of breath, but he looks like any other guy I might see at the supermarket or stuck in a traffic jam.

"Look there, cunt," he says, pushing my head closer to the screen. "Last time I checked, there were 360-odd thousand names on that list, watching our broadcasts. Think of that. 360 thousand men who aren't out there doing what we've been doing, because *we* were giving them what they need. And our girl wasn't even suffering, not really. Used to squirt for me, she did. Creamed like a little pornstar."

The words sicken me, but I stand obediently and listen, like one of his good girls.

"Living the dream, we were, playing with that fucktoy and making plenty of cash from all these punters." He gestures at the screen. "If there's this many secretly subscribing to us through the darkweb, imagine how many more there could be across the world, the ones who didn't find us. A million? A hundred million? *Half the population?*" He sighs. "Shame that such a good thing has to come to an end, really."

I gasp in pain as he tugs my arm so high behind my back that my fingers hit a spot between my shoulder blades. He gives my arm a sharp twist and there's a jolt of agony, a breaching of some kind of boundary, and a hollow snap.

I scream.

"Shut up. That was necessary."

When he releases my arm, I can't move it without feeling blazing pain. He releases my hair and hooks his arm around my throat, trapping my breath. I'm dragged backwards another couple of steps and there is a metallic clunk behind me. He seems to pull me closer to the wall, but then I realise that there is another hidden door, another secret compartment in this dreadful fucking place.

The slightest change in temperature suggests that we are about to descend again.

"Don't be too sorry," the man says. "There's worse ways to go. Down here, the smoke will get to you before the flames do. And at least you'll have someone to snuggle up to while you go."

I feel him drop a few inches behind me, and when he yanks my hair again I can't help but picture Stuart's face, twisted aggressively. I remember the father of my children choking me, biting me, slapping me. I feel my dead husband chewing my labia, as if my most sensitive parts deserve no more tenderness than a mouthful of gum.

The man behind me leans towards my ear and growls, "The world thinks that the sun shines out of your snatches, doesn't it? Everything was fine when you all knew your place, though. Now we can't even discipline you, but you know what? It won't always be like this. We will…"

I thrust my feet into the floor and launch my body backwards. I hear a panicked whistle of breath and brace myself as we fall. The man wrenches on my neck but as our feet leave the ground I feel my skull collide with something. Blood rushes to my head as we plummet backwards and after a short fall I land against the man's sturdy ribs with a crack.

The next few moments are a confusion of tumbled impacts, grunts, and wild flares of pain. His grip loosens on my neck and, using my good arm, I roll sideways. The staircase is too narrow though, and I feel his palm clap against my face.

"*Cunt!*" he shrieks. His fingernails claw at my cheeks and he grabs my nose, squeezing it shut. "Don't you understand *anything?*"

I follow the sound of his voice with the elbow of my good arm, and ram it back into what I hope is the centre of his face. He grunts in pain and his grip on my nose loosens. I twist my body around, wriggling like a serpent with my broken arm crushed against him. I realise that I'm screaming only when I turn and see him wincing and afraid, his nose a calamity of freshly-shed blood.

Despite his obvious fear he manages to grab my hair once again, but instead of allowing him to get a good hold I lunge forwards and sink my teeth into his cheek. He wails as I tear out a chunk of fatty flesh, and in the midst of the horror I marvel at the strength of my own incisors. My attacker pulls my hair but as he tries to drag my head back I lunge again, this time chewing into his neck like a famished vampire. Blood bubbles into my mouth and I taste copper and soapy skin.

He takes hold of my skull in both hands, his eyes tearful and his face and neck crimson. I go to bite him again but he yanks my head sideways. I have enough time to realise that this impact will be unlike anything I have ever felt before, and then I hear the crunch.

My head feels as though it has shattered like an Easter egg.

My vision greys at the edges, but from my leaning position against the wall and above him, I can see his side profile. The back of his skull rests against the edge of one blood-soaked step. He has stopped struggling and although his eyes stare upwards they appear glazed. The hands he holds to his throat do nothing to reduce the blood streaming from his wounds and running from his silent mouth.

Something is wrong inside my head; it's in the slamming of my temples and the skew of my broken-glass vision. I imagine brains peeking out of a split skull. Something irreversible has taken place, and if I don't pull myself up and away from this dying man, I could very well perish alongside him.

Unsteady, I use the handrail to haul myself up.

The man continues to clutch his ragged throat, staring at me as the life abandons him. I only wish that I could make him suffer more, and for the briefest moment I consider thrusting my thumbs into his eye sockets, or stomping his head back against the edge of the steps; even castrating him with my teeth.

I teeter against the bannister, considering my next move, but then see the ring of keys in one of his outstretched hands. He coughs on a viscous mouthful of blood, and with an almost endless wheeze both the air and the life seem to leave him. I crouch and pluck the keys from his fingers, suddenly torn between leaving this charnel house immediately or following a gut instinct.

I feel as though I'm sleepwalking as I descend the remaining stairs. A corridor awaits me at the bottom, identical to the one that had led to the girl's secret room. Have I become so disoriented that this *is* the same corridor, and this is simply the entrance to the girl's room? I totter forwards, knowing that I could fall at any moment.

I reach out and push the key into the lock, and for some reason all I can picture is a cock entering an awaiting hole, a cock that thrusts and savages without consent or concern.

If I open the door and find the girl spooning her dead father I'll tell her, "Sssshhh, it's okay, everything will be fine. All you have to do now that your daddy is dead is let a few more men rape you, with their swabs and speculums and fingers. Sssshhh, good girl…"

The soundproofed door swings wide, revealing another room with the same shape and layout as the girl's. This one, however, seems to contain no pornography, and the ceiling appears insulated and painted a warm beige. The walls bear photographs of a smiling family, a picture of a red balloon floating above fields into the cloudless heavens, and an impressionist painting characterised by sun-scattered waters.

As I take in the sight my head seems to splinter, and with this new agony my legs almost give way. I remember my babies, still alone in the bath where I had left them a lifetime ago. I stagger through the doorway and collapse. I land sprawled before a pair of peach-coloured feet, their pristine nails painted a metallic purple.

"Who are you?" a woman's voice asks. "Where is Jeffrey?"

As the nothingness swallows me, I wonder, has this room always been here, waiting on the other side of the girl's wall?

Jonathan Butcher

27. Girl

I have a window by my bed – that's what you call a bit of screen in the middle of a wall. It's My Window and it's in My New Room.

Being in My New Room is different to when I was in My Room, where I could only see things when I had the light switched on. My New Room is really white, and My Window here is sometimes bright, and sometimes dark. Debbie, the Good Girl who talks to me, told me that when it is dark I should sleep, and when it is bright I should read or watch TV. It's a bit like when My Daddy used to turn my light on and turn my light off, except that when it is dark here in My New Room I can see more than 15 little white lights through My Window, instead of just the red flashing light of Daddy's Eye.

When I had first woken up in My New Room, everything echoed and felt really soft and I wanted to see

Serenity. I couldn't move or see anything properly and they had closed up the hole above my nice smooth cunt. My cunt isn't smooth right now because they won't give me a razor.

Some Daddies came and talked to me, but I screamed, "No no no", and that's when Debbie came. Debbie has short blonde hair, nice white clothes, and I think that she probably has big tits. Debbie asked me some questions, and wrote things down, and shook and nodded her head. I haven't seen any Daddies since.

At first, I could see some other Girls just outside of My New Room. I don't think that the other Girls liked me, especially when I was screaming or scratching the Bad away. Now I'm all by myself and it feels better, even though they keep telling me to put on these long white body-clothes, and I keep taking them off.

I've tried walking around a bit by myself, but there are always two Girls in black-and-silver clothes standing at my door. They don't let me go anywhere unless there's someone else with me, even to do a piss.

The books and the films they show me on the TV at the end of my bed don't show any hard cocks, tight assholes or nice smooth cunts. They usually show Daddies being nice to Girls, and if the Daddies aren't nice they usually go to sleep and don't wake up, or they start being nice to the Girls before the end of the film. If there's any fucking, all you see is the Daddy and the Girl kissing in bed, and then it changes to the next scene.

Debbie gave me a book to read about a little Daddy called Harry, who nobody fucks. Harry goes to a big place where there are people who can lift things up without touching them, but there were lots of things in the book that I didn't understand. When I told Debbie that I didn't understand it, she said, "Here, watch this," and showed me a film with the same name as the book. I think that I understand more of what the book is talking about, now.

The last time that it got dark, Debbie told me that she would have a surprise for me when I woke up. Daddy's surprises were usually a new buzzing toy or a new way to fuck or a new Daddy to meet, but I don't think that Debbie's surprise is going to be like that. I keep scratching the Bad away, and I keep thinking about getting fucked and being burned and hurting, but I feel sort of safe here, at least when Debbie is around. "Mother safe", not "Daddy safe".

When I wake up today, Debbie is sat in a chair next to my bed. She smiles and says, "How are you today, Elizabeth?"

That's what Debbie calls me.

"I'm Good," I say, but my head feels heavy.

"You have a visitor," Debbie says. "I need you to stay calm, if you can. Any screaming, any fighting, any trying to run, and she'll have to leave immediately. Do you understand?"

"Yes."

Debbie goes to the door and lets someone else into My New Room. It isn't Serenity.

This new Girl walks two steps inside. She stands there and looks at me. She is a big Girl, and she isn't pretty, but she has nice green top-clothes and long black leg-clothes. Her eyes go watery, like a Girl in one of Daddy's films. She puts her hands up to her face and I think that she's going to scream but she doesn't. She just breathes out really loudly and puts her hands against her sides again. She says,

"My baby. What did they do to you?"

I just look at her, because she reminds me of My Room back in Daddy's big place. She doesn't look like any of my Daddies, though, and she is too big to have been in any of the films. And she doesn't look like she wants to fuck me, either – she looks like a really, really Good Girl.

The new Girl takes three more steps. "Elizabeth," she says. "Can you speak?"

"Yes," I say, and my arms start to shake, because now I know who she is.

Looking at her makes me think of the hug that Serenity had given me, and of My Daddy saying, "Don't be silly, don't be silly, don't be silly."

I wasn't being silly at all, though. My Daddy was the silly one. It's Good that I hit him with the TV and made all the red stuff come out, and I hope that he never, ever wakes up.

The new Girl reaches my bed. She looks like she feels really, REALLY shaky and different. "I said Good morning and Good night to you every day, after that bastard put me in a different room," she says. "I spoke to you all the time, Elizabeth. I spoke to you through the wall, because I knew I'd see you again."

Her eyes stay watery, and when she holds out her arms I sit up in bed. She wraps me up. I close my eyes.

My Mother kisses my face, and her arms feel like the warmest place I've ever been.

28. Serenity

My head seems to hurt all the time, now. My family is worried about me, but I just need time to adjust.

I've cut contact with dad but I still talk with mum, from time to time. Now that the funerals are over and people have stopped pestering me and asking how things are, I can focus on improving my situation. It's hard to concentrate with all these headaches, though.

Lilith is struggling, but I think she's young enough to cope. I've been making sure to give her extra attention, and prepare her favourite foods as often as I can. I'm sure she'll thank me in the end.

Today, Lilith sits in her high chair with her feet swinging backwards and forwards.

"Yum. Did you enjoy your porridge and syrup?" I ask.

She stares back. She hasn't been talking much, lately.

"I said," I tell her, putting on my best monster voice. "Did you like your yumptious, scrumptious, grizzly bear's breakfast? Nom nom nom…"

Lilith looks as though she is going to laugh, but then her face straightens and she just sits there, blinking, her legs swinging back and forth.

"They're gone," I remind her, back in my normal voice. "It's just us, now."

I refuse to be sad. My parents had looked after the twins while I was in hospital, but mum isn't capable of protecting them like I will and I don't want dad going near them..

"When I come back, we'll play Hide and Seek," I say. "Okay, honeybunch?"

At the stove, I scoop out the remaining porridge from the saucepan. I consider adding some syrup to the bowl, but I think better of it. Only good girls deserve treats like that.

As I leave the kitchen, I have another one of those funny thoughts that I've been having lately. I'm not going to act on them, of course, but it *does* seem like certain tools and meds would be easy enough to find. The tricky part would be avoiding infection.

"Stop," I mutter.

At some point I'll arrange a larger room for my little survivor, but this will have to do for now.

The lamp's wire trails out from a crack in the sealed closet door. I lay the bowl on the floor and put the key into the padlock. When it's open I pick up the porridge and tug the door. Light spills inside.

"Here," I say, adopting a stern voice; cruel to be kind.

My head pounds.

I place the ceramic bowl onto the wardrobe's base and slide it towards Phillip, who is pressed into the corner. The plastic spoon falls out as the bowl spins on the wood before coming to a rest.

Phillip looks up at me, face slack, and pushes a hand into the porridge.

I try to smile, but these days whenever I look at Phillip I also see Stuart, or Declan, or my uncle Ron, or one of the men from the house next door. Part of me wishes that things could have stayed the same, because it isn't Phillip's fault.

It's society.

It's biology.

I watch my little survivor lick fingers that are coated in lumpy gruel, and consider those funny thoughts again. I'm being silly, though. I mustn't do anything rash.

I watch Phillip's glazed expression, licking those gloopy fingers, backed up against the wooden corner of the wardrobe.

On a whim, I decide to try out a new phrase, just to see how it feels in my mouth.

"Good girl."

My voice is strained, but the words seem to make my headache fade.

"Good girl," I say again, and close the door.

ABOUT THE AUTHOR

Jonathan lives and writes in Birmingham, UK.
From the day he was able to transcribe ideas onto paper,
he has been writing strange stories. He hopes he never
stops.

If you want to stay updated with his fiction writing, follow
him here: www.facebook.com/jonathanbutcherauthor
Let's keep things weird.

Jonathan Butcher also appears in the following publications:

The Chocolateman *(from The Sinister Horror Company)*

Flash Fear *(as editor – from Quantum Corsets)*

Death By Chocolate *(from Knightwatch Press/Great British Horror)*

12 Days *(from Burdizzo Books)*

Dark Designs *(from Shadow Work Publishing)*

Trapped Within *(from EyeCue Productions)*

Dunhams Does Lovecraft *(from Dunhams Manor Press/Dynatox Ministries)*

Weird Ales 3 *(from Quantum Corsets)*

The Sinister Horror Company is an independent UK publisher of genre fiction. Their mission a simple one – to write, publish and launch innovative and exciting genre fiction by themselves and others.

SIGN UP TO THE SINISTER HORROR COMPANY'S NEWSLETTER!

THE SINISTER TIMES

As well as exclusive news and giveaways in the newsletter we'll also send you an eBOOK "The Offering" featuring nine short stories, absolutely free.

Sign up at **SinisterHorrorCompany.com**

SINISTERHORRORCOMPANY.COM